D0915592

THE WHISPERING OUTLAW

Max Brand® is the best-known pen name of Frederick Faust, creator of Dr Kildare™, Destry, and many other fictional characters popular with readers and viewers worldwide. Faust wrote for a variety of audiences in many genres. His enormous output totalling approximately thirty million words or the equivalent of 530 ordinary books, covered nearly every field: crime, fantasy, historical romance, espionage, Westerns, science fiction, adventure, animal stories, love, war, and fashionable society, big business and big medicine. Eighty motion pictures have been based on his work along with many radio and television programs. For good measure he also published four volumes of poetry. Perhaps no other author has reached more people in more different ways.

Born in Seattle in 1892, orphaned early, Faust grew up in the rural San Joaquin Valley of California. At Berkeley he became a student rebel and one-man literary movement, contributing prodigiously to all campus publications. Denied a degree because of unconventional conduct, he embarked on a series of adventures culminating in New York City where, after a period of near starvation, he received simultaneous recognition as a serious poet and successful popular-prose writer. Later, he traveled widely, making his home in New York, then in Florence, and finally in Los Angeles.

Once the United States entered the Second World War, Faust abandoned his lucrative writing career and his work as a screenwriter to serve as a war correspondent with the infantry in Italy, despite his fifty-one years and a bad heart. He was killed during a night attack on a hilltop village held by the German army. New books based on magazine serials or unpublished manuscripts continue to appear. Alive and dead he has averaged a new one every four months for seventy-five years. In the U.S. alone nine publishers issue his work, plus many more in foreign countries. Yet, only recently have the full dimensions of this extraordinarily versatile and prolific writer come to be recognized and his stature as a protean literary figure in the 20th century acknowledged. His popularity continues to grow throughout the world.

THE WHISPERING OUTLAW

Max Brand®

GUNSMOKE

First published in the UK by Hodder and Stoughton

This hardback edition 2010
by BBC Audiobooks Ltd
by arrangement with
Golden West Literary Agency

ISBN 978 1 408 46287 4

British Library Cataloguing in Publication Data available.

Printed and bound in Great Britain by
CPI Antony Rowe, Chippenham and Eastbourne

THE WHISPERING OUTLAW

Chapter One

Pursuit

The crimes of Lew Borgen were usually prepared with the greatest care; and having been
plotted with the last degree of caution, they
were always executed by his unassisted hand,
so that there was no need either to share the
plunder or to take another into his confidence,
which is in the end the undoing of even the
greatest geniuses who live outside the law.

But in the case of the robbery of the bank at
the town of Nancy Hatch, Borgen had broken
the first of his rules. That is to say, inspired
rather with "red eye," than with a knowledge
of the ground or of the cash on hand in the
little bank, he had entered the back door of the

7

building in the dusk of the evening, attracted by a light which he had seen in front of the big plate-glass window, with all of its bars of steel behind it.

The back door, however, had not even been bolted, and when he entered the bank, he simply dropped a mask over his face, shoved a gun under the nose of the cashier, and commanded him to turn over the money which was in the safe. He was obeyed, and found himself suddenly in the possession of no less than fifteen thousand dollars in crisp currency. He then gagged and bound his man, departed the way he had come, and, mounting his horse, cantered off up the valley of the Crispin River without attracting the slightest attention.

For two days, then, he pushed steadily up the river, following one of his maxims, which was to the effect that after the commission of a crime one should select a direction and a course for flight and never stop driving straight ahead until at least five hundred miles lay between him and the scene of his last success.

But there seemed not the slightest danger that he would be pursued, and on the third day he broke his rule by halting for some hours to idle in a pleasant little valley just off the ravine of the Crispin.

He was hardly in the saddle again, however, before he saw that he was possibly to pay the penalty of breaking his rules a second time. For he sighted a small cavalcade pushing up the cañon, and they called to him to halt. Lew Borgen did not dare to wait; they were doubtless out to search every unknown man they met in the mountains, so he gave his mustang the spurs and went on up the valley. They followed him hard.

They were so well mounted that if his horse had not been comparatively refreshed by a recent rest, they would have run him down within the first mile. As it was, he drew away to a comparatively comfortable distance, but he soon found that he could not increase his margin. Of the dozen horsemen who had first sighted him, some half dozen had fallen back into the ruck, but the six who remained clung steadily and doggedly behind him, and he could not shake them off.

Borgen began to curse to himself and at himself. This, he told himself, came from breaking his rules, and now he was in danger of paying the penalty. He was so used to making a clean get-away, moreover, that a panic began to rise in his breast. He had his greatest haul lodged safely in the saddlebag which, whenever his left knee pressed it, gave forth a rustling sound infinitely soothing to his soul; but twice as he pushed up the trail that afternoon, the pursuers came close enough to open fire at him with their rifles. Suppose one small pellet of that lead should touch him? What would become of the fifteen thousand, so far as he was concerned?

He saw that it was necessary to do something either desperate or extremely clever. The better blood and bone in those horses which were working up the trail behind him was sure to tell before long, and it was still a bitterly long gap between that moment and the time when the dark of the night would drop over the mountains.

With the very next winding of the trail he saw his opportunity before him. They had been climbing during all of the two days and a half; but during this afternoon the angle of the rise was so great that the horses could push on no faster than a walk. They had left the thick junipers and the level of the yellow and the mountain pines; they were entering the district of the two-leaved pine, and here and there that dwarfed pine which climbs boldly to the timber line.

But though the air was grown thinner and more thrillingly clear, there were still butterflies gleaming over the tops of the grasses, and now and again the drone of a bee came to the ear of Borgen. For it was the end of June, and the sun was gathering strength every day. But, late though the spring was grown, what now caught the eye of the fugitive, as he rounded the bend, was a snow bridge, arched across the river!

Time had been, in the thick of the winter, when a sheeting of ice and of snow had covered the Crispin from bank to bank and stuffed the gorge full as though the glacier age had rolled back upon the mountains, but now the warmer air and the occasional rains and, above all, the hot eye of the sun had thawed the snow covering thin, and then made it break until only a few stiff arches remained. Up and down the ravine, so far as he could look, not one of these bridges now remained except the solitary one in front of him; its brothers had fallen, one by one, into the maw of the Crispin, which went rejoicing among its rocks far below him—so far below that the noise of its shouting was mingled with drowsy and rolling echoes by the time it lifted to the ear of Lew Borgen. But if he could cross that bridge and then break it down behind him, he would have a small but an invincible handicap which his pursuers, he felt, could not overcome.

He paused and dismounted to make a hasty examination. It would not be hard to break down that bridge. The warm winds beneath and the warm sun above had thawed it thin indeed, so that the light filtered blue and cold to the under side of the arch, and from the long icicles which depended beneath the structure the water of its decay was dripping steadily. It was thin enough to break down by dislodging against it any one of a dozen great boulders which leaned down toward it out of the farther side of the mountain. But was it not too thin to bear the weight of his body, to say nothing of the burden of his horse?

11

Borgen looked gloomily back down the valley, around the elbow bend in time to see the pursuit curving around a rock edge of the trail, and he saw that every man in the group was jogging his horse hastily ahead as if realizing that there was a crisis near at hand. There was assuredly no time to doubt and to hesitate, but having risked his life a dozen times before, he must now risk it again without hesitation. He took the reins by their extreme end and led the mustang forward. That wise-headed animal snorted and pulled back, shaking his ears at the precipice beneath him, but Borgen cursed him roundly and tugged him on.

They came out on the bridge, and Borgen set his teeth; for he could not tell whether the grinding and groaning sounds beneath his feet came from the crunching of the hard snow crystals beneath his heels, or from a settling and breaking up of the mass of compacted snow itself. He went on. He reached the thinnest and central portion of the arch safely; he passed ahead, jerking at the reins, and the poor mustang followed, trembling. But when safety seemed only two paces ahead, the bridge quivered violently and then sagged beneath his feet.

The mustang plunged back and drew the reins from the grip of the master; Borgen himself leaped forward with his footing crumbling into the thinnest air. He pitched onto his face, clutched a rough projection, and drew himself up and forward while the snow shelved away beneath his knees. He staggered to his feet and leaped for the firm rock beyond, and as he did so the entire mass dislodged from the edge of the cliff and dropped toward the river. But Borgen was safe. He stood upon the ledge, secure, though so weakened by the shock that now he sank to his knees, and, with the perspiration rolling down his face, listened to the crashing beneath him as the snow bridge struck the river. Then he looked for the mustang.

That lucky brute had managed to get back to the other side, and now leaned, shaking, against the rock, cowering like a human being from the danger from which it had barely escaped. Between them extended twenty-five feet, at least, of nothingness! Borgen was robbed of his mount, that was certain; and worse of all, he was robbed of his plunder also! Fifteen thousand dollars was lodged in the saddlebag yonder. An agony of rage and grief brought the very tears to the eyes of the robber. Only a little longer, and the posse would have completed one half of its work!

It was an unendurable thought to Borgen. He drew his revolver and leveled it. His hand shook like a leaf, so that he gripped his wrist with his left hand, drew a most careful bead, and fired. Oh, lucky shot! The leather which held up the saddlebag was slashed across and tumbled at the feet of the mustang, then rolled over the brink of the precipice and dropped. It

13

struck a narrow projecting shelf of rock, stuck there through an agonizing moment for the outlaw, then staggered off and continued on its flight for the white river beneath.

Before Borgen saw the bag strike, his head was jerked up by the whistle of a bullet and the clanging report of a rifle. The posse was rounding the turn of the trail, and every man of the party was unlimbering his rifle with a yell of disappointment. Borgen shook his big, sun-blackened fist at them, and then whirled to race away among the rocks. Bullets sang about him, but he dodged away like a mountain goat until the boulders were a wall behind him; then he settled down to a steady walk, trying to forget all the calamities which had that day befallen him.

One disaster, at least, had been spared him; among his possessions in the pack on the mustang there was nothing which would serve to identify him; and so far as he knew, there was no one in the world who had ever seen his bare face exposed to the light during the commission of a crime. They could only say of him that he was a rather large man. As a matter of fact, he was half an inch under six feet. The black mask which he wore, and the excited imaginations of observers who saw him in it, freely endowed him with at least an extra inch or two in height and fifteen to twenty pounds in weight. Among his law-abiding compatriots, unmasked and free going, he had never been so much as questioned during his entire career of crime.

He reviewed this comforting thought until his attention was called behind him by the rumble and the crushing of a small landslide. He looked back and saw that the avalanche had been started down the side of the mountain by the foot of a running man who was in plain sight, heading along his trail; and behind there were others, four of them!

It was the posse again. For one dexterous fellow had noosed a rock on the farther side of the gulch, and then the lightest of the party had handed himself across the chasm along the lariat. Once across, he had only to make sure that the rope held fast on the rock to which the noose end was fastened. Then the rest of the party followed, with the exception of the eldest and heaviest, who remained behind as a guard for the horses. The others then broke along the trail of the fugitive, found his sign easily, and so came in view of him.

To big Lew Borgen it was the end. He was nearing forty, and though he was strong as a gorilla in his arms, his legs were useful only to grip the sides of a horse. Those agile fellows who were coming on his trail would run him down as easily as a pack of greyhounds at the heels of a panting bulldog. Yet he could not even turn and make a worthy fight for his life, hand to hand. He was armed with one miserable revolver only, and the others, as they ran, slung rifles in their right hands. The minute he paused to make a last stand, they would simply drop to their knees, well beyond all random range of the revolver, and riddle him with bullets.

That was not their purpose now, apparently. They knew that the game was now entirely in their hands, and they were determined to take their prize alive and so hand him on to the powers of the law.

So there remained to poor Borgen only the use of those legs, so bowed and crooked by a life in the saddle, that when he ran it was like the swaying efforts of a fat old woman. He struck away valiantly, however, going straight up the mouth of a gorge which now narrowed rapidly. He was being driven into a trap, he was assured, but his lungs were burning now with his efforts, and he was so miserable that he hardly cared when the chase ended.

Presently he rounded a turn in the ravine and saw that his way was blocked indeed! Before him arose the wall of a terminal moraine of a glacier which, in the old days, had flowed in a river of ice down the gorge, hewing it as it went, and then had joined that large mass of snow which had ground out the cañon of the Crispin.

It was a sheer wall which it presented to Borgen. For some reason that moraine was not the rounded mound which he had so often seen; it rose above him almost perpendicular.

Certainly it would be perilous, but it was not absolutely impossible to scale it, perhaps; for the moraine was composed, on this front, at least, of a rubble of stones of all sizes. He threw himself at his work and began to clamber up, a chill in the small of his back as he thought of the bullet which was sure to plow through his flesh and stop his upward progress.

Chapter Two

Scaling the Cliff

Borgen was not now so awkward as he had been when he was running, for now the strength of those long and dangling arms, ridged and ribbed with muscles, came into play, and he swung like a sailor up the face of that crumbling cliff. He dared not pause to think of what he was doing. Most of the handholds which he secured were upon rounded stones, threatening to slip off at any instant, and he wedged the toes of his boots into the smallest apertures. He had started hopelessly, but now as the face of the rubble slid beneath him, he began to wonder if luck would not aid him, indeed, over the very brink of the precipice; for having won so many times when he was cornered might he not win still again? Tomorrow he would boil his coffee at a lonely fire and laugh at this adventure!

That pleasant thought had just occurred to him when a rattle of voices struck him from beneath, and he knew that the pursuers had come in a group around the last bend of the little gorge. They rushed on nearer him, and the climber, expecting the hiss of the bullet, found his breath coming in short gasps. A pair of brown wings flirted in his face—he could not see the bird or recognize it on account of the perspiration which was rolling steadily down over his eyes—but, ah, how divine a gift it seemed, to be able to wander through the world at will, regardless of paths and of cliffs and of mountains, living in the thin air!

He could hear their voices, now, rolling up to him like hollow sounds from the bottom of a well.

"Has he run on plumb into the side of the mountain, boys?" they were calling to one another. "Here's his trail, and here's where it ends."

"Scatter out on each side. Of course he ain't melted into stone. Maybe the fool is trying to hide on a patch of them bushes."

It came dimly home to Borgen. They had not even thought of raising their eyes to scan the face of the cliff, so improbable did it seem that any one could have attempted to scale that upright wall. Trembling with joy, he resumed his work, carefully now, for a single stone dislodged would be death! By the voices, by the faint sounds of their heels grinding the rocks, and by the light jingling of their spurs, he knew that they had scattered well to either side, and now there was far less chance that they would spot him with their eyes.

He went up with an uncanny deftness. Now the top was near. Now the edge of the cliff with the blue beauty of the sky was almost in touch of his finger tips. Now he swung himself joyously over the ledge—alas! It was a mere depression in the face of the cliff, and there still remained a full twenty feet of climbing, with his strong arms trembling and aching from that last swift effort.

From the comparative security of that ledge he looked down. At once his head swam. Only a bird, it seemed, could have perched safely upon some of those rocks which he had used as a footing. Then, sick and trembling, he let his weight fall forward against the rock, but with no sense of security, for what had seemed to him an almost comfortable ledge and resting place the moment before, was now no better than the sheerest portion of the wall beneath him. It was only the dread that his fear might become greater, that made him force himself on. Could he have descended that cliff front, now, he would have called out to the posse below to rescue him, and then take him prisoner if they wished. But they could not help him; only some winged creature could be of avail to him—like that little brown bird, multiplied into one a thousand times greater.

Upward he went again, no longer confidently, but with a terrible weakness of wrists and elbows; all the nerve strength was exhausted from them, and he shuddered each time he changed a handhold. He had covered more than half of the way to the top from the ledge, however, before the great calamity happened. Under his right foot a stone gave way and bounced down the face of the cliff. Now was the time to rush the concluding part of his effort! He had hardly the height of his own body to go to reach the topmost rim of the cliff, and a few bold efforts would place him there—in safety!

But the weakness of fear had run through all his body. He was hanging at the length of two quivering arms, and the strain was coming on the shoulder sockets; terror took his breath, and he began to strangle and gasp for air.

Then there was a heavy impact beside his face, and a flying fragment of rock struck his cheek and was imbedded there, the point driven in almost to the bone, and causing him an exquisite agony, all the worse because he had no hand free to pluck it out. The clanging report of the rifle rolled up the rock to him. As if by magic, the fear was swept from the body of Borgen, and his weakness passed away with it. He pulled himself up hand over hand with uncanny swiftness. So sure was he of himself and his powers, that he even swung himself from side to side to baffle the aim of the riflemen below.

All their rifles were chattering at once, each repeater humming until the steel of its barrel grew hot. They had two handicaps working against them. In the first place, they were suddenly looking upward, squinting into the dazzling brilliance of the sky and trying to strike a dark form against dark rocks; in the second place, and more important, they could see that their quarry was marvelously near the upper rim of the rock, and they were in a nervous tremor of haste to land him with a bullet which would make him throw his hands wide apart and hurtle backward through the air, turning slowly over and over until he landed lifeless at their feet.

So they pitted the face of the stones with a hundred bullet scars, but Lew Borgen tugged himself up to the edge of the cliff, kicked up his heels, and swung himself to safety. He whirled about at once and emptied his revolver at them, cursing and snarling. He was not a good shot, but one lucky try went through the boot of a member of the posse. He leaped for cover, hopping upon one leg, and yelling in his agony. It was too much for Lew Borgen. He rolled upon the ground, hugging himself, and shouting with laughter until a stabbing pain in his cheek reminded him. He drew out the bit of stone from his flesh, looked at the reddened point curiously, and then rose to face the sober work which lay before him.

First of all, it was necessary that he at once strike out toward a point at which he would be most apt to secure a good horse and a saddle. And he must steal that horse—for he was broke! He stopped and ground his hands together. He had had a small fortune in the instant before; and now his hands were empty, and he had to steal a horse. It was the one thing he had vowed that he would never do; he would rather murder a man, by far.

"By the heavens!" cried Lew Borgen, throwing up his two long arms, "I ain't going to steal no hoss now! They can find me and they can hang me fust, and be damned to 'em! I ain't going to be that low!"

This resolution filled him with a sort of ecstasy of courage and power. He strode on vigorously, crossed the crest of the range in the dusk of the day, and dipped into the night toward the desert beneath him, which was blackening when the summit was still in the alpenglow.

He came to the lower slopes, and among the foot-hills he reached a ranch, found the barn, found the shed where the saddles were kept— even spotted in the starlight a tall gray gelding in the corral—a horse after his own heart. But Lew Borgen stuck to his oath. He felt, in an

23

obscure way, that he was making a bargain with fate, or luck, or God—whatever one chose to call the ruling power in life—and that having refrained from stealing a horse, luck would refrain from striking him down.

Then, with a mild pleasure in himself, he went into the ranch house, stole an ample back load of provisions, and having stocked his cartridge belt with ammunition, retreated into the night again.

He made a small fire between two rocks, cooked coffee, ate some bacon between slices of bread, and rolled over in the sands for a sleep.

He did not need an alarm clock. For though he was half perishing with exhaustion, yet he knew perfectly that the subconscious self which watched over him would rouse him in case of peril coming near, and that he would waken when the time came to march.

Waken he did while the stars were still bright, before the first hint of the coming dawn. He did not look to his watch, as a lesser man might have done. Neither did he groan in the cold of the morning, or because his head was ringing and whirling with an ache, but instead, he rekindled his fire, reheated some of the coffee left from the night before, drank enough to have poisoned any ordinary man, and tramped away upon that day's journey.

How long would it be before he drank coffee again? For he could not carry with him the pot he had stolen from the ranch house. He prepared philosophically for the struggle, and though he had never before made a journey of any length on foot, he struck away at a steady pace and maintained his gait throughout the day. He kept within the line of the foothills, just as a wild beast, coming down from the heights, will lurk among the hills for a long time before it ventures onto the plains, where mere speed may prove more formidable than sheer striking power and skill in battle—where the wolf tribe is more dreaded and more at home than the cats.

It was a bitter march for Lew Borgen, but he stuck manfully by his guns until the dusk came. He had been marching a mighty total of hours, and even such a poor walker as he had by dint of painful patience set many a mile behind him. Then, as he came over a hill in the early evening, he dropped suddenly upon his face as though a bullet had felled him, for in the hollow beyond him he saw four men riding with rifles under their knees and their heads high, as are the heads of men who are hunting a crafty game.

They rode onto the next hilltop, and thence they surveyed the country, but they did not see Lew Borgen, lying not fifty yards away and praying that no dog had accompanied the party. Finally he watched those bodies, so clearly outlined against the brightness of the west, sink into the dark of the hollow as into a black lake. Borgen rose wearily to his knees and rested there a while, slowly rubbing his aching legs; for he knew that these fellows were hunting no animal inferior to man, and that he was the object of their great solicitude.

He did not grin as he thought how he had escaped them. Mounted as they were—and how bitterly well he remembered the gaunt and racy outlines of those cow ponies—they could drift about through the night as softly and as swiftly as the terrible loafer wolves. They could comb the hills in circles, hunting for him, and there was no doubt as to the final issue. They would catch him beyond a shadow of a doubt.

So Lew Borgen surrendered. He went up on the top of a hill, kindled a fire to make him warm—for a sharp wind was cutting down at him from the snows on the mountaintops above—and waited for that signal light to draw his enemies in upon him. In the meantime, he ate a supper joylessly and then rolled a smoke. But it seemed that the very boldness of the situation of that fire had robbed the man hunters of all suspicion.

It was a full hour after it first flamed before a voice spoke behind him.

"Steady, Borgen, and don't look round!"

Chapter Three

A Mysterious Schemer

Mechanically, strangely without emotion, Borgen pushed his hands above his head. What he was deciding at that instant was that when he was taken to the jail he would make a clean breast of the whole story—leaving out certain unfortunate affairs where he had been forced to kill his man—and startle the authorities by the detailed list of his crimes. How the papers would bulge with the copy they gleaned from him! The Sunday supplements would flare with color for the sake of Lew, and many a cowpuncher up and down the range would mutter thoughtfully: "Well, I'll be darned! It was Lew Borgen, was it?"

27

"Steady, Lew," the voice behind him was saying, coming nearer and nearer, though without the slightest accompanying sound of a footfall. "You don't have to keep those arms up. I ain't troubled about that when I got the drop of a gent from behind. But just sit quiet and look to the front."

Then Lew Borgen thought of something else. How could this stranger in the darkness know him? For certainly his face had not yet been seen. How could it be, unless in some fashion his identity had become known, and the whole world had already spotted him?

"How did the news blow round that it was me?" rumbled Lew, dropping his hands accordingly and removing the cigarette from his lips. "Who got the tip that it was Borgen that done the work?"

The strange voice answered, and still in a murmur which had a secret quality in it, as though this soft-footed person dreaded lest any one should overhear what he had to say. Indeed that guarded speaking voice had the quality of a whisper.

"Nobody knows except me, Lew Borgen. If anybody else knowed, I wouldn't be here. You wouldn't be no use to me."

"Nobody but you? Who the devil might you be?"

"A friend of yours, maybe."

"No friend of mine has a voice like yours. But if you're a friend of mine, for heaven's sake lend me your hoss to beat it before they close in on this here fire."

"They ain't closing in on this here fire," replied the other. "They ain't half interested in closing in on this here fire."

"Are they all drunk—or sleeping early, then?"

"I'll tell you how it was," said the other. "There was a hoss stole out of a corral about three miles from here, about half an hour back. That hoss was saddled and bridled and sneaked out of the corral, and then along come a cow-puncher, seen what was happening, and give the alarm.

"The whole bunch says: 'It's that crook getting him a hoss.' They hop out and feed their hosses the spur as soon as they get into the saddle. They get going fast enough to see the way the crook was heading, and they seen that he had a lead hoss with him, in case that the other one should give out.

"Pretty soon the sheriff and all the boys that was hunting for the robber, they all hear about the chase and start heading in. But though the hoss keeps right on running, there ain't any rider in the saddle. He's picked the wildest hoss in the corral, and one that ain't been any more'n half broken. When he gets a mile from the ranch, he hops out of that saddle and gives the hoss he stole a cut with his quirt, and that there mustang ain't going to stop running inside of a hundred miles, and the boys will be busting their hearts right along its trail all the time."

He paused, chuckling softly. "And then," he

went on, "I came straight back to you, Borgen, to let you know that you can take my hoss and ride on after you've had a sleep to-night."

"In the name of heaven," muttered Borgen, "who might you be that would give a gang a run like that for the sake of helping me out?"

"Don't worry about me," said the other. "I saved you because I wanted to use you. I seen that you was about to get your neck stretched——"

"That's a lie! What they got agin' me that would get my neck stretched? Trying to throw a little scare into me, partner?"

"I'm telling you the truth. The cashier died, Borgen. The sight of that gun of yours was too much for his bad heart. He dropped half an hour after you left town. I think they'd hang you for that, don't you?"

"I didn't know," whispered Borgen. "I didn't know."

He rubbed his face furtively, but the blood would not come back under the cold skin.

"Well," he said, "how'd you manage to spot me?"

"I've spotted you for a long time. I been following you, Lew, and watching your methods!"

"Say, partner, who the devil might you be? Will you open up and tell me?"

"I'm a gent that's going to turn into a business man, and the business I'm going to follow is your line, Borgen. That's why I've saved your neck tonight."

"H'm," muttered Borgen.

"I've followed your trail for a long time, from the Tuolome robbery to this last little affair——"

"What? Who hitches me up with the Tuolome case?"

"I do, Borgen!"

"This here is a trap, but you don't get me to talk. I'm mum. I wish to heaven I could have a look at you!"

The other laughed. "I saw the whole play," he told Borgen. "I saw the man drop. When he tumbled, he reached out, and his hand grabbed the shelf and pulled it down on top of him. You put that shelf back, and all the things that went on it, before you went through his pockets. Seemed like you was more cut up about knocking that shelf down than about killing your man."

Borgen remained agape, for an instant, staring into the darkness. He was realizing many things. He had always thought that the reason he hated to have his crime traced was because he feared the penalties of the law, but now he saw that it was even more because he did not wish to have the shame of his guilt known to a single human being. With all the energy in his soul he was wishing to whirl about and pump a bullet into the body of this quiet-spoken man behind him, and so rub out the one eyewitness.

"I've learned some very important things from watching you," continued the stranger.

"I've learned, for instance, that it is above all foolish for a man to have partners in crime if he wishes to go along without being caught up. Because one partner will be pretty apt to turn State's evidence if he gets in a pinch. Ain't that right?"

"Are you trying to pump me?"

"I'm telling you facts, not asking you questions. In the first place, I say, a gent has to play a lone hand. That's why you've worked for ten years without being spotted a single time."

Borgen started; then he set his teeth and flushed. It was maddening to think that this stranger, whoever he might be, had been able to throw a light upon all his past.

"But," went on the man behind, still keeping to that secret and cautious tone, "the trouble is, it looks to me, that a gent that plays a lone hand ain't going to make no big killings. Look at yourself. You've robbed fifty times. You've never been caught once; you've never even had your face seen. I don't know of a record like it in history!"

"There ain't any, son," said Lew Borgen proudly.

"But how much money have you today?"

"I've made plenty——"

"That's not straight. You've only made one big haul, and that was the last one. The others, you've bungled, or else you've played for small stakes. You've taken a lot of time, but you haven't taken time enough, d'you see?"

"Maybe you know," sneeringly replied Borgen.

"I'll show you I do before I'm through with you!"

A little silence fell after this remark; a screech owl passed startlingly close overhead with a whoop.

Then the stranger continued: "Now I'll tell you a plan that's worth a million!"

It was an odd plan indeed. He unrolled it slowly, carefully, answering a hundred questions with perfect patience, until the whole details were in the hands of Borgen. This rider in the darkness, this strange and crafty fellow, had completed an outline for a new system of depredations. Having noted that the lone agents were those who succeeded in escaping without detection, he had also noted that the profitable crimes were those in which a partnership was made use of. One or more men studied the lay of the land, got on the inside of the "lay," as it were, and then their confederates arrived, and the job was completed, after which the whole party decamped.

The plan of the night rider was much more complex. He himself determined to be the head of a whole gang of marauders. But many of these would not even be known to one another. A dozen tried and hardened men, all of them past the flush of restless youth, were to be enrolled in the plan.

These were to be located in a number of

different towns among the mountains, some of them in pairs, some singly, according to their temperament. These were to work up the details of the robberies, planning every inch of the ground with the greatest care; and when a plan had been perfected, it was to be communicated to the lieutenant—the man who had secured each of the rogues, and who also passed on the orders of the invisible chief.

"But how," broke in Borgen at this point, "are you going to keep unknown to me? If I'm the lieutenant, I got to see you, don't I?"

"You'll never see me except at night, and you'll find me masked and talking soft. Would you know me tomorrow, Borgen, if you heard me talk nacheral?"

Borgen had to admit that he would not. Having received the details of a plan, the lieutenant was to pass the word on to the chief, who in turn would select two or three men, as many as were needed, from some most distant point in his chain of towns and bring them, when all was prepared, swiftly across the mountains to the place to be struck. Then, having committed the crime according to the carefully detailed plans of their confederate, they were to sweep away out of town, but their confederate remained quietly behind in the town until all the fuss had blown over, after which he would quietly start away, and go to the place where he was to receive his equal share of the loot—perhaps a month after the crime had been committed.

Every bit of plunder was to be equally divided among the entire gang, except that the chief was to receive three shares, and the lieutenant two.

The beauty of the plan was obvious. To put the matter on a large scale, one man planned a crime in Arizona, communicated his scheme to the lieutenant, Borgen, in Idaho, who gave it to the invisible chief at one of their regular meetings. The chief looked over the scheme, and, if he approved, took two of his operatives from Montana and swept south some two thousand miles to the little town in Arizona. There they completed the carefully planned work at a single stroke, and then sped north as fast as they had come, using the railroads wherever possible.

"Because what is a hoss good for?" said the night rider. "Except to get himself caught by other hosses?"

There was a truth in this which Borgen could not deny.

In fact, the more he pondered the scheme, the more perfect it seemed to him. There was not to be a wild orgy of crime. Each man would not be asked to plan a crime or to take part in the execution of one, more than once a year, in all probability. In the meantime, he could reside in one locality, if he chose. He could build a home, marry, raise children—all of this was possible. The invisible leader, in fact, told Borgen that he would have in his service none saving men close to middle age who wished to have dollars rather than excitement.

"Suppose that the gents won't fall in line?" asked Lew Borgen.

"You know a dozen up and down the ranges," said the man in the night, as calmly as ever, and without leaving that singular hushed murmur in which he chose to speak. "There are Tirrit, Monson, Nooney, Doran, Anson, Lambert, Oliver, Champion, Montague, and others who are outside of their spring days and ready to settle down, except that they been drifting so long that they ain't got the nerve to start in with honest, steady work. Well, Borgen, when you come and talk to them, they'll listen. Every one of 'em knows that you been on the crook, but they know that you been smart enough to keep folks from talking about you; you never been pinched, and that counts. I tell you, Borgen, it ain't a question of whether they'll come in, or not; it's only a question which ones we want to ask. Spot the ones that I've told you about and come back inside of a month. Come back four weeks from tonight and tell me how things have gone.

"Here's a hoss that'll carry you; not a very big one to look at, but a mighty man-sized hoss for you to ride. He learned mountain climbing from the mountain goats, and then throwed in some tricks of his own making to improve on 'em. He's a gold-plated wonder on a narrow trail, friend! Take this hoss. Inside of the saddlebag you'll find a wallet, and inside of the wallet you'll find three hundred dollars in honest money. Take hold of that money and spend it like it was your own. It'll pay your expenses until you come back to me four weeks from tonight."

He patted the horse's mane.

"But how," exclaimed the robber, unable to suppress the cry, "how'd you know that I'll come riding back here inside of four weeks when I got your hoss and your money to use for my own? What makes you trust me, stranger?"

There was another little pause; and this time, when the voices ceased, they could hear a coyote wailing faint and far upon the very horizon of sounds.

"I'm a judge of men," said the stranger at length. "I look at a gent's face, and then I know what to expect out of him. I know what to expect out of you, Borgen, and I know that you'll play square with me!"

Chapter Four

Facing the Whisperer

Borgen had not known that he was a man so esteemed among the brethren who lived outside of the law, but everywhere he went he and his plan were well received; from Champion, that agile little black-eyed ferret of a man, famous for a hundred robberies, to big, lumbering Anson, celebrated for the killing of the great "Kid" Jennings, all the men who were listed to him by the nameless fellow in the night listened to his plan with the keenest interest, and, without an exception, they subscribed their strength.

Doran summed up their opinion: "This here is what we been needing. It's an age of combinations, ain't it? There's corporations for every-

38

thing. And here we start up our corporation, too. Who in the devil can this gent be? Maybe it's old Thomas? By the heavens, I'll bet it's him. He was turned loose from prison about three months back!"

Every one of the elected, in fact, had an opinion as to the identity of the stranger, but Lew Borgen was past guessing. He hardly cared, for as he progressed from place to place, a new and greater thought had come to him. Suppose that he were to make this nameless progenitor of the scheme stay outside of the workings of the plan? Suppose that he, Lew Borgen, were to constitute himself the unseen director of crime and be the lieutenant to himself? For one thing, he would be then the recipient of five shares—two for himself and three for the man who did not exist. In order to carry on his scheme safely, he had only, it seemed, to shoot down the originator of the scheme at their second meeting. In that fashion he would himself become the fountain head of the work. There would be the great advantage that while so much glory would go to the phantom, all the blame would also go to the invisible idea of a man who no longer existed, and Lew Borgen, as the mere transmitter of orders, could not be attacked for the failures.

The more he contemplated that position, the more ideal it seemed to him, and when at length he approached the scene of the rendezvous, his mind was fully determined. He waited among the neighboring hills until the darkness had fallen thick and black across the sky. Then he left his horse behind him—that same wiry little goat of a horse which had turned out to be worth all the praise which "The Whisperer" had bestowed upon it—and started forward on foot, after stripping off his riding boots and drawing upon his feet soft and soundless moccasins. It would go hard indeed if, so equipped, he could not steal upon his man unseen and unheard. To guide his approach, there flared the camp fire of The Whisperer upon the hilltop!

What a fool yonder schemer was, for all of his brains!

"That," said Lew Borgen to himself, "is the trouble with all these here brainy gents. They can do a pile of thinking, but that lets 'em out. They ain't no good at working out the details. Me, I'm different!"

Borgen saw himself already rich. Within a year of this systematic plunder, he would be able to retire with his gains to some far-off quiet place.

He went onward, crouched low, the revolver ready in his right hand, sometimes steadying himself with his left hand against the boulders over which he was passing. Now and again he paused to study the fire in front of him. There were a number of wavering shadows around it, some of them were rocks, and one must come from the form of the man of the night.

"Steady, Borgen," said a terrible and familiar murmur behind him. "Steady, man. If you turn, I shoot."

Borgen straightened himself by jerks until he was erect. His blood was racing, and yet he was cold from head to foot. In the same jerky fashion he began to realize what he had done—how he had repaid the generous kindness of his benefactor with an attempted treason—a most foul murder! He waited for his death. He wanted to whirl and attempt to fight it out, but the steadiness of that soft voice had made it impossible for him to stir, it seemed. He was chained to the spot.

"Stranger," he started to say in a husky voice.

"Be quiet, Borgen," said The Whisperer. "I understand. This is what I expected. This is what I wanted you to do. Do you think I'd have any value or any respect for you, if you'd just gone blindly ahead doing what I told you to do? You'd of been a fool, then, not a man. Them that think—them that keep trying to improve themselves and their chances—them are the kind of men that I want around me. The way you laid in them moccasins—that showed foresight, Borgen. I sure admired to see that!"

Borgen dropped his gun to the ground and then turned halfway around; finally he turned again and faced The Whisperer for the first time.

"It's all right," said the latter. "I don't aim to be seen by many folks, but you and me are going to meet a thousand times, and here's where

41

you might as well begin to get used to me."

Borgen grunted. He had not yet made out what was in store for him; but he was certain that he was being tantalized with a cruel irony, and that in the end the pellet of lead must crash through his brain. In the meantime, he stared until his eyes ached at the figure before him. He saw a man not more than middle height, with shoulders so exceptionally wide that he seemed rather short. He wore a wide-brimmed hat, his face was a black shadow of a mask, and for the rest, there was nothing to distinguish him from a hundred other cow-punchers. He was not Thomas, that was certain; neither was he half a dozen of the other guesses which had been made about his identity.

"Light a cigarette," said The Whisperer. "Then we can start in and talk free and easy."

He added: "But first pick up your gun and slide it into the holster. Only—after it's in there, don't disturb it none, Borgen!"

Borgen obeyed. He noted with a grim amazement that the man before him had sheathed his own weapon and did not bother to draw it again while Borgen raised his own. But the hand of The Whisperer hung close to the butt of his Colt, and it seemed to Borgen that there was power in that dangling hand to strike him with a thunderbolt. Slowly, slowly he raised his gun; and at last he pushed it harmlessly home in the holster just as he had been ordered. In that brief instant he had accepted the superiority of The Whisperer forever, and it had become impossible for him to strike in his own behalf. He was subdued utterly.

He rolled his smoke, and The Whisperer did the same, with such adroitness that he had scratched his match before the other had completed his manufacture. Lew Borgen began to study his chief by the light of the match. It burned blue till the sulphur was gone, then the clear yellow flame sprang out and showed The Whisperer with dazzling clearness against the velvet black of the night. He seemed even broader of shoulders, more wedgelike in build than he had been in the dark. His hands were slender. His face was completely hidden behind the black mask. But between the side of the mask and the crown of his hat there was a curl or two exposed, of brilliant red hair.

The heart of Lew Borgen leaped. It was "Red" Murray, then! No, he decided an instant later, it could not be the celebrated Red. That worthy was a full two inches taller than The Whisperer. Neither was Red capable of a scheme of such fine proportions. Neither would he have been able to read another man's mind as The Whisperer had truly read the mind of Lew.

"It worked out like a charm," said The Whisperer in that same voice, which was indeed not a whisper at all, but a barely audible enunciation. It was hardly as penetrating as a whisper; it lacked the sibilant sharpness of the latter, which carries far, even though the words are not audible.

"It worked out like a charm, Lew. You got them all in line, I see."

"How the devil do you know that?" blurted out Lew, stung into speech by his impatience. For such omniscience was like a weight upon his soul.

"Why," explained the leader, "that ain't hard to make out. There's nothing spooky about me, Lew. I knew my scheme had worked out, because otherwise, you wouldn't of come back to murder me on account of it. When I seen you sneaking up the hillside, I knowed right off that you was paying me a mighty big compliment without being right sure of it yourself!"

The other shrugged his shoulders. This explanation had at first seemed to simplify matters a great deal and to explain everything, but the more he pondered upon it the more worthy of thought it seemed to him. Such cleverness was even more than mysterious—it was a terrible thing.

"You was watching for me to come at you— from behind?" he growled out, forcing out the words of his shame.

"Oh, I knowed where you'd come," said the other calmly. "They ain't no doubt that a gent has to try to improve himself when he gets a chance, and here was a chance for you to get rich quick. With the cream of the plunder rolling in, and you getting five shares out of eighteen or twenty——"

Lew Borgen was crushed to the very ground; this seemed to give proof that the other had actually the power to step into the minds of others. For had that not been the very inner thought of Lew when he planned the assassination of his chief?

"What name do I call you by?" he asked suddenly.

"Whatever you want. I'd rather stay without a name."

"Well, then, d'you mean to say that you still want me—after all of this—to stay on as your—lieutenant?"

"Of course," said The Whisperer. "Look here, Borgen, ain't it better the way it is? Now you know a little more about me than you used to. If I took another gent, I'd have to go through all of this again. It'd take time, and it'd be trouble. I hate work, Borgen. I sure hate laboring!"

Borgen drew a long, slow breath. He began to feel that he had entered the service of the devil indeed; and he would just as soon have attacked Satan in person as to have raised a hand, after that instant, against The Whisperer. Yet, when he tried to explain it to himself, he had to admit that the latter had neither drawn a gun, fired a shot to demonstrate his skill, nor even raised his voice with threats. It was odd, indeed. But Borgen felt as though he had come from facing cannon when he left The Whisperer that night.

45

Chapter Five

Tirrit Talks

There was no tidal wave of crime, of murder, and robbery. Here and there, separated at distances of five hundred or even a thousand miles, crimes were committed which were carefully prepared with a painful and laborious hand; and then they were executed in an instant by one or two bold spirits who dashed into a town, did the work for which they had been appointed, and sped away again. Sometimes they struck at night; but sometimes they shot in and out upon their mission in the daylight, securely masked. No one could say that there was a single method in these crimes, for each of them was committed in a totally different fashion, having been planned by a totally different head.

But for six months nothing was known to the public, or, for that matter, to the busy police themselves. They simply were aware that there were more crimes this year. There are always crimes which go undetected, for a time, at least; and the police are not impatient. They endure a world of abuse and contempt, but when the time comes, they do their work and go on without cheering. They have no bands and battle flags to raise their spirits high for their struggles, but each man goes over the top by himself, in the dark of the night. The police, then, knew that there was a slight increase in the number of unpunished crimes, but the increase was small.

No one would have guessed that a new and incredibly successful band was at work had it not been for an accident. A certain eminent rancher, the owner of numberless acres, cows by the thousands, farm land along one rich river bottom, and many an irrigated desert acre— a man of untold wealth in fact—was riding over his domain one day when he came upon a horse standing beside a prostrate man, in a gully. He thought at first that it was one of his lazy cow-punchers taking an afternoon nap, so he spurred his horse ahead and galloped to the place.

Percival Kenworthy, for that was his name, found a wounded man. The bullet had apparently gone straight through the heart, but this was only in appearance, for it had glanced around the ribs and lodged in the poor fellow's back. He was unconscious. His pulse was fluttering on the verge of extinction; plainly he was close to death. So Kenworthy forced a dram of brandy from his saddle flask down the throat of the dying man and was rewarded suddenly by a gasping voice and opened eyes. He was a stranger to the rancher, but he knew his good Samaritan at once.

"Kenworthy," he gasped out, "listen to me. I'm Tirrit. Ask the sheriff. He knows me—too well, maybe. I'm dying. Him that killed me was——"

Here his eyes grew dull, and he passed into unconsciousness again. Kenworthy, feeling that a terrible revelation was about to be made, applied another dram of the powerful drink. It recalled the wounded Tirrit again to consciousness, and he picked up the story where he had left off.

"The Whisperer killed me!" he murmured.

"What about The Whisperer?" asked Kenworthy.

At this the eyes of the other grew dull with despair, as if he realized that there was more to tell than he had time and strength to relate.

"All them robberies——" he began. "The safe cracking at the First National in Deaconville—the clean-up in Lead City—twenty others; they was done by one gang, and The Whisperer runs that gang. Me—I was one of the crew. But they got me. The Whisperer got me. I was trying to find out who he was. I *did* find out! And so he plugged me. His name——"

His voice choked away. With a feeble hand he drew the rancher's ear down to his stiffly struggling lips.

"The real name of The Whisperer is——"

What that name was, the rancher could not make out. It was only a confused gasp of breath, and then Tirrit died. But Kenworthy had the body brought into town and carried his strange tale to the sheriff. And, just as Tirrit had suggested, the sheriff knew him only too well. Tirrit was young. He could not have been past thirty, but it appeared that he was old in crime. He had spent half of his years since he was eighteen in prison. The other half he had sustained himself with crimes of a dozen sorts. Moreover, the sheriff knew all about the clever work which had resulted in the cracking of the safe in the First National Bank in Deaconville. He knew, also, of the clean-up in Lead City; and he frowned in sober intensity of thought at the news.

Not only that, but he entreated the rancher to say nothing of his experience or of what he had heard from the dying bandit. Too much publicity would destroy the chances of the police to run down the criminals.

In the meantime, the worthy sheriff got in touch with the officials of neighboring counties and neighboring States and passed the word to them. He himself went to Lead City and then to Deaconville, and, with the aid of the local authorities, used his best efforts to discover similar methods and the work of the same master hand behind those crimes. But they were very different. They were as entirely unique, so far as one another was concerned, as if they had been conceived by two entirely separate minds.

Yet all officers of the law know that the majority of criminals, even the greatest of them, perform their crimes according to one pattern. Having achieved their first real success in breaking the law, they continue until death to duplicate that first great effort. Here, however, was all the evidence of two distinct minds conceiving, and two distinct hands in the execution. The police were disturbed. Some of them went so far as to openly state that they discredited the dying statement of Tirrit. It was simply an effort of dying malice to make trouble for a companion whom Tirrit hated, and who had shot him down in a fair fight.

All that really resulted from this careful examination was that the rumor spread abroad. Knowledge shared by so many men could not be kept secret. Indeed, it is the nature of a secret to make men desire to talk about it. The most harmless gossip, if it be told in a whisper, will immediately be exploded into public attention. So it was with the tale of Tirrit's dying story. The noise of it shot abroad upon the thousand invisible wires of rumor, and straightway other men who dwelt outside the law heard of it.

The tale wandered to a hundred resorts of crime——somewhere in the West a great band was operating. Its exact location was unknown, but at least it was certain that it operated, or had operated, in that great county of mountains and desert where the rich man, Percival Kenworthy, had established his ranch. So, toward this focal point the powers of the world of crime began to draw. Wild fellows with ungloved right hands and bright eyes and faces as sunburned and lean as hawks, started over the mountains and through the desert.

They found no Whisperer ready to enroll them in a secret gang when they arrived, but they did find one another. Straightway they pulled together in threes and half dozens. They began to strike right and left. They rustled cattle. They blew safes. They worked as footpads in the towns and as holdup artists and plain highwaymen in the open roads. The carnival of crime which the plans of The Whisperer had so carefully avoided, came into birth within a month after the death of Tirrit. By a cruel trick of fate, it was Percival Kenworthy who suffered more than all the rest.

He was not a man to sit still and endure such a life, having his cattle driven off by the hundreds, his payroll intercepted on its way out from town, his foreman "stuck-up" in the very shadow of the bunk house. He took the matter into his own hands. He called a meeting of his neighbors, the most representative citizens from the mining district in the mountains, the lumber camps, the cattle ranges, and the near-by towns.

Fifty sturdy men of affairs gathered under his roof for dinner to taste the excellent whisky of the rancher, to partake of his fine fare, and to see lovely Rose Kenworthy, newly come home from an Eastern school. For she presided at one end of that huge table while her father presided at the other.

At that dinner they made much talk, and in the end they elected an active committee of a dozen of their ablest members to go to the sheriff and ask to be allowed to participate in the suppression of the crime wave. Kenworthy, of course, was the chairman who went to the sheriff and offered the aid of the citizens in the campaign against The Whisperer. For, since that mysterious name had been first mentioned, it was constantly in use as the guiding spirit behind every crime.

Had he possessed a dozen bodies, he could not have been in every locality where crimes were blamed upon him. That name became a fascinating illusion. Every bank robbery was laid to his name; and every hobo with sore feet and five days' whiskers on his face was arrested and gravely given the third degree to see if he might not be the master criminal.

The Whispering Outlaw

"No one," said Kenworthy to the sheriff, "has been able to spot the master criminal. I propose to forget that name. I propose a great crusade against crime in general, throwing out a great dragnet. When we haul it in, The Whisperer will be one of those entangled in the meshes."

He cleared his throat. He was a pompous man who wore a stiff white collar even when he was riding on the range. He talked even to his daughter in the quiet of his home as if he were making a political speech from a stump, and he had a way of tucking his rather small chin inside his collar, thrusting his hands into his coat pockets, spreading his legs apart, and delivering his thoughts upon the right way to carve a goose with as much passion as an old, ranting actor doing the closet scene in the third act of *Hamlet*.

The sheriff did not smile. For Kenworthy was too rich and too successful to be smiled at. He was never referred to in any of the local papers saving as "our distinguished neighbor," or "the cattle king," or, "one of our most distinguished citizens." To laugh at such a man was apt to have cost the sheriff five thousand votes at the next election! For the rancher secretly owned a controlling share in some three or four of those papers which most assiduously mentioned his name. So the sheriff duly swore in Kenworthy as a deputy and gave him the authority to enlist others in the name of the law.

Immediately the "crusade against The Whisperer" began to be a serious affair. There were virtually pledged to it some thirty or forty of the strongest men on the range, each of whom could throw three or four well-mounted, well-armed men into the field for a campaign of any duration, without missing their hands from the working forces upon their ranches.

Deputy Kenworthy found himself placed at the head of a hundred hardy fellows who knew the range to a T, and who were keen as fox hounds on the trail because each one of them was promised three months' pay in a lump sum if he could strike down or capture any man who was afterward proved to be a criminal. Kenworthy hardly knew how to dispose of such large forces, but he was one of those men who could take advice even when trying to give it; if he wanted to know how to build a skyscraper, he would have called upon an eminent architect and started giving him his own ideas until the architect in wrathful self-defense blurted out a few of the truths concerning that matter.

So Kenworthy now went around and talked to some of the old-timers who had been members of vigilante committees, and it was not long before he learned from them that the best weapon of all against crime was that simple name—vigilante! It was of such a power that the strongest bands of criminals and outlaws melted away before it; it had a marvelous prestige, and was known never to have failed in the past. Deputy Kenworthy swallowed the thought at once, equipped his crusaders with the name of vigilantes, and started out to mop up the country.

He mismanaged it sadly. He left holes a mile wide in the nets he spread. But, nevertheless, he had a hundred sharp-eyed fellows working for him, and they began to turn in results in spite of Kenworthy's blundering methods. They caught one rascal of a cattle rustler; they nailed a horse thief; and then they caught a yegg, an old and expert safe cracker. What they did to him was not pleasant to relate, but the group which caught him consisted of old, hard hands, and they determined to make the yegg talk. They tied him to a tree and toasted his feet until he fainted over the fire, and when he recovered his senses the sight of the flames made him begin to blab all that he knew. It was enough.

He gave them names and places as fast as they could write them down. They spent three weeks of furious riding, wearing out a horse and man every other day, but at the end of the three weeks the crime wave in Kenworthy's county was suppressed with a vengeance, the jails were packed, and suddenly it was as safe to walk the open highroad as it had been dangerous before.

Just as the campaign was closing, the time of the county election rolled around, and in noisy admiration of the rancher's work, he was rushed into the office of the sheriff at the last moment, by a tremendous vote, to his own bewilderment and infinite gratification. So he gave a dinner in his big ranch house to celebrate the end of the crime wave and the beginning of his term as sheriff. It was a very happy affair. Men arose one by one and told him what an eminent man and public benefactor he was, until the face of Rose Kenworthy was crimson with shame, and the face of her father was crimson with happiness. At length he rose in turn and announced that he had at least put an end to the crime wave and that The Whisperer would never be heard from again.

"Because, gentlemen," said the rancher, "somewhere among those whom we have caught in my dragnet—somewhere among the rascals whom my vigilantes have brought in, is that arch-rogue who dared to show his face among us in this county of—ours."

He had almost said "mine," but saved himself at the last instant.

"The Whisperer," he continued, "is dead; and may he never rise again!"

This toast was drunk with cheers, so loud that they made a shadowy figure which was at that instant stealing downstairs into the new sheriff's cellar, pause and listen. But presently he went on again. He reached the bottom level of the cellar and searched the wall deliberately with his pocket electric torch. The faint glow thrown back upon him revealed the fact that he was completely masked, his head being hung in black all round. He examined the wall until he discovered something to his interest upon the plain surface of the bricks. He began to fumble at one of these, finally drew it forth, and then inserted his hand into the aperture which it left. At once there was a sharp click followed by a rolling noise of the most oily smoothness; and a section of the wall, a full three feet wide, swung softly open and revealed, within, the lofty and glimmering face of a steel safe.

With the utmost satisfaction, the masked man surveyed it. Then he raised his head and listened with the greatest apparent content to the noise of mirth which continued above him and which was audible even to the faint chiming of the glasses, now and then, because of some door which was left open into the dining room. He now closed the door of the vault behind him almost reluctantly. He laid forth a quantity of yellow laundry soap, excellent for rough cleaning and excellent, also, for the construction of those molds which yeggs run cleverly around the edges of the door of a safe, so that nitroglycerine may be induced to flow around it and trickle into the crack of the door, no matter how narrow.

He next produced a small flask which those of the "trade" would have guessed at once to be filled with the "soup." And, having laid forth these articles, he looked over the safe with the greatest deliberation. He laid his hand upon its bluff and rounded corners as though he admired with all his heart the solidity of its workmanship and the exquisite strength of the tool-proof steel itself. Then, having completed his survey, he set suddenly to work to make his mold of the soap.

Chapter Six

In the Clearing

The explosion had rather a force than a noise.
It took hold on the house like the hand of an
earthquake and made it shudder. At the same
time an almost soft and puffing noise of the
explosion was audible not so much through
the house itself as in the distance around it,
where the sound traveled through the thin, pure
mountain air and made every cow-puncher in
the bunk house sit up, bolt erect, to listen and
to wonder. In the dining room upstairs, every
guest and the wise host himself sat staring, glass
or cigar in hand for a frozen moment.

Then: "A lifter!" muttered someone who had
been a miner in his youth.

"An explosion!" cried Sheriff Kenworthy. "By heavens—it can't be———"

The last thought had turned him white and so stunned him that he was unable to complete the utterance of it aloud, or even to himself. Neither could he move. During that precious interval there was only one person in the room who stirred, and this was Rose Kenworthy, herself. She had not let an instant go by in idleness, but after the report she slipped from her chair and ran to the door, where she listened to the quivering echo like that which follows the passing of a man with a heavy tread. Then she ran back to one of the astonished guests.

"Bud Chalmers," she cried softly to him, "that came from the cellar where my father keeps his—Come! Let's see what's there!"

He had to take her arm and draw her back, or she would have led the way in person, as though she preferred such an adventure and such a risk to the scene which she had been forced to sit through in the dining room.

By this time the whole group of men had turned in a body, and they rushed down the stairs, poured into the cellar, and found a broad dark mouth yawning in the cellar wall. They streamed in, guns in hand, electric torches quivering with eagerness. What they found was the floor of the little room strewn with a litter of papers, the door of the safe lifted cleanly from its mighty hinges, and the interior of the safe entirely gutted. It brought a wailing cry of almost childish rage from the newly famous sheriff. He fell upon his knees in front of the safe, and threw out his fat arms. What he might have said would never be known, for the slender form of Rose darted to his side.

"Dad," she whispered in his ear, while her strong young hand sank into his soft shoulder, "they're watching you—you'll die with shame if you don't act like a man now!"

It brought him to his feet. He was able to muster a roar as he turned to his posse, and then pointed to the door which opened at the rear of the cellar.

"That's the way, boys," he cried. "That's the way that dog went! Let's ride him down—five thousand in cash to the man who drives a bullet into him."

"Look here!" cried someone.

He turned the round, bright eye of his torch against the wall of the cellar and there they saw, white and new, a great "W," inscribed in careless scratches.

"The Whisperer!" came the cry of a dozen men. "The devil has dared to do this while we upstairs——"

Flushing with anger, they glanced to one another. In truth, The Whisperer had chosen to make a mock of them, and there was no doubt about it. While they drank honor to the sheriff and scorn to the baffled outlaw, he was proving that their dragnet had not touched him at all by actually plundering the safe of the chief

61

of the vigilantes, with all of his men scattered about.

They stormed from the cellar; they found their horses; they stormed out from the house in a great circle, some riding toward every point of the compass, and in this fashion one man sighted a gray horse in the moonshine, half lost among the shadows of overhanging trees. He shouted a challenge, whereat, the other put spurs to his horse and galloped across the fields. At once the hue and cry was raised. They flogged and spurred their horses forward furiously, on the trail of the other, who aimed his flight straight for the neighboring cañon mouth, and was immediately lost in the woods which crowded it.

In the meantime, they had hardly disappeared when there issued from the little room in the sheriff's cellar where the safe was kept, and actually from behind the safe itself, that same masked robber who had dared to insult the power of Mr. Kenworthy in his own house. He left the cellar leisurely, strolled to a knot of trees near the house, and there mounted a horse which had been left in concealment. He now struck away at a swinging gallop, whistling softly to himself, and riding rather as one who enjoyed the rhythm of the gallop than as one who needed desperate speed to save him from a great danger.

But as for the posse, they rode with a wild unconcern for the nature of the ground over which their horses flew. There is nothing that makes a man so utterly reckless as an affront to his vanity. Not a man there but would have gladly lost half his blood for the sake of sinking a bullet into the body of The Whisperer because of this night's insolence. They gave their horses wings, and they were quickly upon the very heels of the fugitive. Only the thick screen of the trees kept them from riddling him with bullets, for they were constantly in short revolver range. They might have run him down almost at once had it not been that he had apparently carefully planned the way of his retreat, and dodged from one narrow avenue in the woodland to another, so that they were several times lost for a moment and gave up valuable rods of ground before they caught the trail again.

Foremost among them galloped Rose Kenworthy herself. Not that she carried a gun, or that she could have used one, but she would not be left behind in a hunt which was more exciting than ever a fox hunt in the world! She had a saddle upon her tall bay gelding before the others were fairly under way. She flew two fences and caught up with them as they twisted across the first fields, and after that, she was in the very front, though her father swore and the other men begged her to go home. But Rose, being an only child, had of course been terribly spoiled; she did not even think of obeying them, but she cantered on, cheering her horse along and shouting with glee as she swung right and left to dodge the low-sweeping boughs of the evergreens.

The big bay went lame suddenly. He stumbled, almost fell, and then slowed to a walk.

"Now go home!" shouted someone darting past at full speed. Which of course determined Rose to stay on that trail if she had to go forward all night on foot. She flung herself from the gelding's back while the hunt slid past her and went crashing into a thicket beyond. She turned the gelding loose. The poor fellow would find the best way home to his stable and at his own speed, which would be better for him than leading. Then she started to tramp forward with her throat closed and her heart huge with wrath. To add to her fury, the way was interlaced with many entanglements of roots, and every now and then she tripped and almost fell upon them. Twice, indeed, she actually plunged forward upon her hands and skinned them on the gnarled bark or the stones on which she struck.

Who, in the midst of a ranting argument, while pacing back and forth, has tripped and stumbled? Who has stubbed his toe while promenading with the greatest dignity? Such things are nothing to small mishaps while one is in a passion; and Rose Kenworthy would have taken mountains in her hands and smashed them to pieces against one another, so wild was her passion of temper. When she scrambled to her feet after the second fall, she paused and stamped and beat her stinging hands together in impotent fury.

"Oh," cried Rose, "if only I were a man—if only I weren't such a—such a——"

She could think of no fitting word, and so she strode on over the cushioning mats of needles with her fists clenched and her eyes rolling among the shadows; the noise of the hunt had died out far, far before her, and the knowledge that she was doing a very foolish thing in following them only increased her rage and her determination. So it was, coming out into a little clearing in the forest, she was amazed to come on the scent of a cigarette. She looked about her in the deepest astonishment, but entirely without fear. That emotion, in fact, was well-nigh a stranger in her composition.

She was in a forest of huge yellow pines, and the light of the moon struck down in spots here and there across the woodland. There was some distance from the ground before the big first branches began, and Rose could look far away down avenues of brown columns, with silver spots of the moonshine falling here and there, quite regularly, upon the pavement of fallen needles. To her it seemed a windless night, but pine trees will tremble with air currents which the human skin cannot detect, and in the stillness of the atmosphere all the needles were astir and made a faint and ghostly hushing sound.

A little rivulet was not far away, raising a merry bubbling and calling as it tumbled over the edge of a boulder into a pool beneath, and through that thin and pure mountain air the sound struck across the cañon and was rung faintly and deeply back in echo from the opposite wall of the little valley; so that it seemed there was another waterfall in the distance, a thundering giant whose strength was just beginning to make the air tremble.

This was the scene, and these were the sounds in which Rose found herself when that poignant and rich fragrance of the tobacco came to her and scattered the tatters of her passion away, and poured upon her mind the holy water of that mountain quiet.

She could see no source of the smoke at first, and then she saw, in a patch of the deepest shadow, the figure of a man sitting with his back to her, cross-legged upon a great stump, as quiet as a stone, or a meditating Indian. Nothing about him stirred except his right hand, from which the silver curl of the smoke went upward as he brought the cigarette to his lips and carried it away again. His head was bare. His face was raised toward the sky as though he peered out from his shadow upon the brilliance of the moon, which was now rounding into the three quarters, and drowning all the stars in her floods of silver. From his head, raised in this fashion, long black hair fell away—hair almost long enough to touch his shoulders, and cut away in a thick, sharp stroke at that point. It had a striking effect.

The Whispering Outlaw

Indeed, there was everything about his attitude, his immobility, his black, long hair, the thinness of his face—for she could see the prominence of his cheek bone and the hollow line of his cheek—to make her think that this stranger was truly an Indian. Yet she knew that he was not, before she saw him fairly.

She herself had not moved from her place after first coming into the clearing; but the stranger suddenly bounded from his tree-stump chair as though shot upward from springs. He landed upon his feet, facing her, and at the side of a tree trunk, behind which he disappeared. In no longer a time than it takes the camera shutter to wink back and forth, this picture was rubbed out, and she found herself alone in the clearing.

There was a little touch of fear in her, then. But she shrugged her shoulders and forced that weak sensation away. Then she crossed the clearing and followed a curious impulse which made her sit upon the stump just where the stranger had sat, and raise her head. But having done so, she did not see the moon or the sky. She closed her eyes to all of that. Instead, far up the cañon she heard the noise of the racing man hunt as it thundered along at the heels of its prey.

Apparently the cliff faces on either side of the valley were so placed by a freak of nature that they reflected all the sounds from the upper valley as mirrors will repeat light, and focused them, faintly to be sure, at this particular point. But how could this long-haired stranger have known the thing? Where was he when the hunt rushed past, sweeping across this very clearing? Suddenly, she knew that the black-haired youth was standing just behind her, watching her as still as a stone!

Chapter Seven

Listening

There was no doubt about her fear now; it froze her in a great cold wave; but like all people who are naturally very brave, the touch of fear simply startled her at once into action, and, jumping down from the stump, she whirled about and faced him. For her instinct had not been wrong; he had been standing just behind her, and he was still there, his arms folded, his black hair falling around a sun-darkened face, very thin, and oddly handsome. He was not a small man, but so slender of foot and hand and standing with such a strange lightness, that he gave her a singular impression of fragility. He might be in age anything from twenty-two to thirty, for he was one of those odd people upon whom time, during youth, leaves only negligible traces.

From the instant she faced him she lost all her fear; there remained in her only pity that so weak a creature should be living here in the forest like a wild Indian; for Indian dark though his skin was, he had the regular features and the great and open eye of a white man; and if there still lingered in her blood a little chill of that first strangeness in his appearance, it merely sharpened her attention.

He was dressed almost in rags. He wore tight-fitting trousers of deerskin, after a vanished Indian fashion, and even the leather had been worn almost to tatters by his rough life. Upon his feet were moccasins. He wore a shirt of which the sleeves had apparently been worn to bits, so that now they had been trimmed off nearly to the shoulders and exposed his long, narrow arms, as sun-browned as his face.

After this second and closer survey of him, what seemed wonderful to the girl was that he should have ventured to come out again and have faced her, for his whole air and manner was one of the most perfect aloofness. He had folded his arms and looked at her so quietly and steadily, that he might have been thought to be viewing a species of strange plant, an oddity in trees, rather than a human being. Rose was very distinctly uncomfortable. Her early pity died away. She found that she was forgetting the tatters in which he was dressed, and she was unconscious of anything about him saving the large, clear eyes and the thin face, so cleanly carved, so carefully made.

"What are they hunting?" he asked her. "Why are they running in the middle of the night? Have they rounded up a mountain lion? Surely they don't run the lions without a pack of dogs!"

The clearness with which he enunciated, the ease of his speech, all told a great deal to Rose; it meant an educated mind, and that a man of education, perhaps of real and fine culture, should be existing in this guise in the woods was more wonderful than ever.

"It's a robber who broke into my father's house," she told him.

He seemed to pay no attention to one part of what she said, but was the more shocked by the other half.

"Is it a man they are hunting? Are there really people who ride after others all night—as if they were beasts?"

"Don't you understand?" she told him. "This robber broke into my father's house and took away thousands of dollars."

"So they are going to take his life for that. Well, if you had a million of dollars, could you make a new life? Could you buy it in a market?"

She decided that his brain was a little touched. "You've come up here to spend a summer close to nature?" she said, abruptly turning the subject.

He waved his hand, though she could not tell whether it was to brush away her conjecture or assent to it. But she had an ample stock of assurance. She was one of those girls who unite with the flower and loveliness of a woman the sharp eye and the steady hand of a man; and she talked to the stranger with the intellectual confidence of a cow-puncher who has an enemy covered with his Colt.

"When I saw you at first," she told him frankly, "I thought that you were a wild Indian."

He shrugged his shoulders as though her conjectures did not interest him, and it occurred to Rose that he acted as though he was actually becoming bored.

"I was listening to the hunt," he said coldly. "From that stump you can hear everything in the valley, almost. All the ground noises and all the tree sounds and all the winds speak out of the valley to this place. The walls are sounding boards, you know; and they focus here. You can hear everything on the edges of the valley, too. It's a sort of a listening post, you might say."

He stepped to the shattered stump and rested a hand upon it, raising his head as he had done when she first saw him. His eyes closed; his face relaxed as utterly as perfect sleep.

"Now you can hear, of course," he said, and beckoned her to him. She, also, leaned across the stump. What she heard was the whisper of the wind among the pines, and, in the near distance, the dying scolding of a squirrel which had been awakened by the rushing of the horsemen through the night. There was the dull and melancholy voice of the little waterfall, also. But she knew that the man beside her was hearing other things. Presently he began to explain.

"That wolf you hear calling up the valley," he said, "is the old she-devil with only three toes on her left forefoot. She was murdering calves on the Wilson ranch a week ago; they ran her up to the summits, or very nearly there; then gave up the chase. Now she is coming back!"

"Were you on the Wilson ranch a week ago?"

"I was near."

She held her peace and thought the more. The Wilson ranch was a matter of a hundred and eighty miles away, and the intervening region was a tumbled and jagged mass of raw rocks and steep-browed mountains, all giants. To have traveled that distance upon foot, as the outfit of the stranger suggested that he had done, to have crossed those knife-edged rocks with moccasined feet, was truly marvelous. Quickly she estimated that distance. Then she turned to the subject at hand. She had not heard the cry of the wolf; and even now, though she knew from what point to expect it, and though she strained her attention, she could not hear a sound comparable with the devilish wailing of a lobo.

73

"There!" he said suddenly. "The noise of that hunt frightened him almost to death." He chuckled at the thought. "He ran as fast as he could run, and you know a mountain lion can go faster than the wind for a little distance. But now he's got his courage back; he's coming down the valley again. Listen to the silly fellow warn every creature in the mountains that he's coming! He's telling them all to stay in their holes or up their trees on the thin little branches where he can't get at 'em. How he's booming now! Sometimes I think that that rolling thunder of his so frightens them that they are frozen. Besides, the echoes pick up his voice so fast that I suppose they hardly know from which direction he's coming, and if they try to run, they may dash right into his jaws."

She was growing worried. He talked as if the very air trembled with the roaring of the hunter, and yet her own keen ears did not hear a sound. She told him so, and at this he replied by taking her wrist, not with a foolish familiarity, but with fingers as steady and as cool as a rock; there was a suggestion of strength, too, in that touch, which made her able to understand that gigantic march across the mountains.

That wonder passed quickly from her mind. It was as though this strange fellow were saying: "Listen! Listen!"

No doubt it was simply the effect of absolute quiet, rocklike stillness of body and brain, yet it seemed to her that something flowed into her from the cool fingers, and all the borders of her mind were enlarged, her senses were purged from a mist. The fragrance of the evergreens touched her with a new and stinging sweetness, the cold of the mountain night wind passed into her very blood, and then into the dim borders of her consciousness were borne new sounds, first a faint and far-off wailing which made her shudder—that was the cry of the wolf coming down the draw; then she heard the cry of the mountain lion.

Contrasted even with the feeble voice of the waterfall they were sounds as faint as the shining of a new moon compared with the blaze of noonday, and yet they were clear. He released her hand; and instantly she heard the noises no longer. She might explain that through her sudden excitement and the quickening of her heartbeat, and yet she told herself that there was something more which could not be explained. Though she was as calmly practical as any man, yet she found herself believing that here was a mystery beyond explaining.

"The wolf has heard the lion hunting," said the stranger. "One last yell—you hear it?—and now he is silent and goes sulking off on a new trail, I suppose."

She watched him sharply, but there was no affectation of the charlatan about him. He was as little excited as though he had simply called her attention to one of the neighboring trees.

"How long have you lived like this?" she asked him suddenly.

"I don't know," he answered. "Four or five years, I suppose."

"Four or five years! In these mountains?"

"Yes."

"I've never heard of you."

"You and the others live by day," he said. "That's why they never see me. Except for the fur traders, you're the only person I've talked to in all the times I've been here."

"You've grown lonely, then?"

He hesitated. "Tonight—after I saw you—but only a little. You see, I've had the fear always that sooner or later I'd be pulled back to my own kind. When I watched you from the trees it seemed to me that I was surer of that than ever before."

It was only a suggested compliment, but it pleased her wonderfully; she could feel her heart softening toward him every moment they continued their talk.

"Then I saw," he continued, "that I'd have to come out and talk with you. Otherwise you'd go home and tell them that you had seen a wild man in the woods and they'd start out to hunt me—just as they're hunting that poor fellow far away—far away yonder in the draw. Listen! They're shooting. Perhaps that means they've cornered him. Perhaps that only means that they're giving up hope of getting him and they're firing at random in the hope of bringing him down."

She listened and heard nothing; but had he touched her, she had a perfect confidence that she could have made out the distant fusillade clearly enough.

Chapter Eight

No Mystery

In that short pause she stepped back and looked at herself and this stranger in perspective, so to speak, and what she saw she wondered at. She had an almost irresistible desire to know more of him, to mine down toward the very roots of his heart and find out all the emotions which actuated him. Other men she knew were interesting enough; but here was one who offered a real problem if she would even faintly comprehend him. Something was missing, too, which should be there. She was only beginning to see what it was; another man would not have been able to stay so long with her in the dark of the forest, with the spotting of moonshine like fallen silver here and there, without making pretty speeches.

She detested compliments, perhaps because they had always fallen to her share in such abundance, and more than once she had found herself wishing that her face were plain; then she would be taken for her real worth, and beauty, surely, is a matter of flesh only. However, there was no question of pretty speeches in the stranger. He talked to her as though she were a man, and in spite of herself she could not say that such a conversation was exactly to her liking. As for the hunt of the robber, she had not the slightest interest in him.

"But do you think," she said, "that having seen you and talked to you, you are any less strange? Do you think you are like other men?"

"No difference in the world," he assured her, almost with irritation. "There's not a shadow of mystery about me."

He broke off to say in a whisper: "There's a little bright-eyed rascal of a Douglas squirrel peering at us from that branch yonder. I'll make him talk!"

He whistled a bar or two of a song which was vaguely familiar to her, as though something she might have heard her grandfather sing in her infancy. The moment his whistling ended, from a great branch near by, a squirrel began to bark furiously; then fell as suddenly silent.

"No one can be lonely with such talkers around, eh?" murmured the man of the forest, and she wondered at him more than ever.

He went on calmly: "That's why I came out to talk to you," he said; "to show you that I'm just like other people, except that I have a few different habits. Then I thought that you might be willing not to talk about me. I thought you might promise that, if I were willing to answer any question you cared to ask. Because I know that it's only things we're half familiar with that seem worth gossiping about."

"I have no right to ask you questions; I have no right to inquire into your life," she said, flushing.

"And I have no right," said he, "to ask you not to tell other people that you saw a queer man living like an Indian and acting like an idiot. I've no right to keep you from sending twenty riders and a pack of dogs on my trail— for my own good, to bring me in where I can be taken care of."

He made a grimace.

"Well," she said, tormented by curiosity more terrible than the hunger for forbidden fruit, "suppose we strike the bargain, then. I'll give you my hand that I'll never mention your existence; and in exchange you'll tell me who you are and why you are here."

"It's so simple you may be tempted not to believe. But you see, I promised that I'd show you that I'm no mystery. It's all as straight as a string, and a very short string at that!"

At this, he rolled himself a cigarette, slowly, shaking his head a little, as though he found it hard to believe that the former self upon which he was now staring could really have been his flesh and his blood and his brain. He lighted his smoke, and then told his story.

"I was living in a big Eastern city," he told her at last. "I was fighting two enemies, a failing business and consumption. They beat me together. On the same day I failed for a small sum, but just enough to bankrupt me, and then I went to a sanitarium where the doctor made me strong enough to sit up at the end of six months. He told me that what I really needed was a year or two of clear, mountain air. 'But I suppose,' said he, 'that your business will not let you.'

"As he said it, he struck a weight from my shoulders. All through my sickness, as a matter of fact, I had been tormenting myself with the problem of how on earth I could go back into the harness and pull out the wagon of my affairs which was stuck so deep in the mud. Suddenly, while he talked, I took a new view of the whole affair. What was business to me except ruin? Why should I not go where I could live freely? He advised me to keep away from the excitement of men. Why not a life in the wilderness?

"So I tried it. I raised enough money to pay a passage West, and at this end of the line I bought a rifle, a revolver, ammunition, a few simple traps, some coffee and some bread, and I started out to make my living. It wasn't easy at first. I didn't know how to fish, or how to shoot, or how to trap. I was so ignorant that I had to find a new way of learning. What I did was to start studying the animals I had to live on by hunting.

"Because, if I wanted to have meat, I had to get almost close enough to it to touch it, before I could be sure that my shot would bring it down. The result was that I studied them day and night—but chiefly by night. After all, I was a meat eater, a beast of prey. And when do the other beasts of prey go out to hunt? They go by night, of course. So I used to say to myself in those days—they were wonderfully hungry and wonderfully happy days, too—I said to myself: 'I am a mountain lion; and I must do exactly as it does, except that I shall not be so foolish as to make a noise while I hunt, and that I shall use a leaden bullet instead of teeth and claws for bringing down my prey. Aside from that, I must learn how a mountain lion hunts."

"How terrible!" murmured the girl, and, she added: "And wonderful, also!"

"But it was not from the lions that I learned the most," said he. "My chief tutor was an old grizzly with more wisdom packed away in her old head than any dozen men I have ever known. I follow her every year. When I come across her trail it's like meeting an old friend. As long as I have followed her and studied her, I never come near that clever old veteran without learning something new.

"She's a rascal, of course. I suppose most very clever people are. She's a cattle killer, you know. But she's not like most of that sort of bear. She kills cattle, but only now and then when other provisions run low. It's exactly as if she understood that it's a dangerous business to venture onto the fenced-off lands of men. After she's made a killing, and eaten the animal, she heads for the highest mountains with her cubs and lives on insects and roots and rabbits above timber line for a while, keeping a lookout all the time.

"I learned from her how to trail and how to hide my trail. Because, of course, she used to know that I was following her, and she would leave me trail problems enough to have baffled an eagle. They always fooled me. It was really ridiculous. That half a ton of ambling bones and meat could fade away out of the landscape and leave me with three days of devilish worry and work to find her again!"

He paused to laugh, silently. She wondered over him more profoundly than ever. But he seemed to have forgotten her, so intent was he on his tale of bruin.

"When she went to sleep that first winter of my stay in the mountains," he said, "there was a very great deal which she had failed to teach me. But still I had copied out of her book enough to keep me busy all winter rehearsing and digesting. Over an area of a thousand square miles she had taught me every stream, and where the best shallows were for fishing; she had taught me the little pools and the lakes in the same way. She had charted for me the districts where the bees were the busiest; and she showed me a thousand places where one could make one's trail vanish into thin air and where one could take cover. She taught me all the wise ways of the chipmunks so that I could never really be hungry if I had the patience to do a little digging; and if I wanted to be absolutely sure of a good meal every day, I'd carry a pick and shovel with me, not a rifle. Roasted in a certain way, you know, there's nothing more delicious!"

He drew in his breath as though he were famished at that instant.

"You know," he continued, "a grizzly is really a very studious creature. I thought during the first season that I was doing nothing but copy bruin. But in the second season that I trailed her, I found that she was constantly hunting *me!* Upon my honor, the old rascal was actually playing on my trail just as I had been playing on hers."

"Good heavens!" cried the girl. "Do you mean to say that the terrible creature was hunting you down?"

"Just as I was hunting her, of course. I had no right to hound her as I was doing, and she knew it. Very naturally she looked into the matter after a time, and I suppose that the clever old girl was delighted beyond telling when she found out that there was actually in the wilderness something from which she could learn a few lessons which would make life easier for her, now that her bones were growing brittle and her muscles stiff. I give you my word that a hundred times she has laid in the brush and watched me make a fire. And a hundred times she has walked around and sniffed at me while I slept."

"And you didn't die of fright in the morning?"

"We were fast friends long before that. We were silent allies, you know. I never saw her for long at a time; and we never talked to one another. But still we kept in touch. Oh, if I could tell you how I have watched her dig out a nest of chipmunks and gobble them as they came to light—and if I could tell you how she watches me fish! She has pointed out the best pools and streams for the work, but she doesn't bother to fish a great deal now. When she's hungry for fish, she gets on *my* trail. She knows that when I fish at a pool I'll be sure to leave three fourths of my catch on the banks, and when I'm gone she comes out and gobbles up what's left.

"She has an appetite to amaze you, you may be sure! Last year she was cornered by hunters and badly smashed up with bullets. I found the place where she had cached away herself and her cubs, and she and they were starving because she was too crippled to hunt for a whole month. So I did the hunting for the whole party—it kept me busy day and night, and even with my rifle and my traps, I could not take enough to give her more than a lean diet."

"You actually fed her?"

"I left the stuff where she could get it."

The girl was silent, full of thought.

"That gives you an idea how I have lived," said he. "I came out here ignorant and helpless, and the beasts taught me how to get food. They kept me from loneliness. They showed me the mountains. Above all, they showed me that night is the time to live. I learned to sleep from prime to mid-afternoon, just the way Madame Bruin does. That left me the morning and the evening, which are the richest times of the day, and then the whole night, for hunting or for trapping. Of course I need a little money now and then for odds and ends and for guns and ammunition. So, in the heart of the winter, I trek north and trap for foxes. In two weeks I catch enough to do me. I take the pelts down to a Canadian fur trader, here or there, and they cheat me to their hearts' content, but even so I get all the money I need, and more.

"Besides, they don't ask questions. I'm not so very different from some of the half-breeds who come into the posts looking wild. They ask no questions, take the furs, give me a third of their value in cash and half their value in trade, and then I'm off again for the southland. And that, I think, tells you what I am, and how I live. But you can ask me whatever you wish. I'll answer you frankly."

He had finished the cigarette, put it out carefully, and waited, folding his arms. But she was too bewildered to speak at once. What he referred to as a simple narrative seemed to her the wildest romance to which she had ever listened or ever read.

"If there is nothing more," he said, "au revoir, mademoiselle."

"Wait! Wait!" she called to him as he turned away. "Are you to go like this? Am I never to see you again?"

"We have made an agreement," said he.

"That you will answer my questions. There are a thousand I have for asking, but they are all swirling in my brain. I haven't them in order. But tomorrow——"

"Tomorrow I must be far away."

"Why must you leave?"

"It is foolish to make a long hunt in one place. I have been here for two days. Besides, I have grown hungry for honey, and I know a place a little distance away where there was a great swarm last year. It should be a mine of good eating this summer."

"But if it is close——"

"Fifty miles, I think. A good days' march to the southwest."

Fifty miles in one day—fifty miles of such mountains as these for a single day's march! She looked at him in amazement. And yet it was not impossible. The frailty which she had first thought she noted in him was deceptive, after all. It was mere lightness of a body strung with sinewy muscles, tireless as a wolf on the trail.

"It can't be this way," she said. "I have to see you once more. Then I'll release you. You can go where you please after that! But—I'm going to make a list of things to ask you when I see you again."

It seemed to her that he sighed in the little pause that followed.

"If it must be," said he, "I am unable to disagree, you see."

"Where can I find you, then?"

"Where you please. I shall come."

"So long as it is not near other men, I suppose."

"That is no difference."

"But if they found your trail——"

He shrugged his shoulders and laughed again, as silently as before.

"They will not follow it long," he said. "If a thousand-pound grizzly can make her trail vanish, why cannot such a little thing as a man do it? I promise you, if Madame Grizzly used to make trail problems which I could not solve,

I now make ones which she cannot decipher. I am very proud of that!"

She wondered at him in silence, and then: "Good night!" he said, and was gone, gliding away without a sound, though he stepped upon the noisy pine needles which, when she herself walked, crackled continually under her feet. She felt like a great and clumsy creature as she turned back toward the ranch; she was a mundane being indeed compared with that form of shadowy lightness.

Instead of holding straight for the ranch house, however, she followed an impulse which led her to the right, through the forest, and up to the crest of the ridge which walled in the cañon to the westward, and as she stood on the eminence, she saw a shadow slide out from the trees not a hundred yards away and pass down into the valley. It was a man, running with a swift and yet an easy stride. It reminded her of that frictionless lope of the wolf which goes on and all through the whole of a day and never wearies from the dawn to the dark. This was the man of the forest.

Then she remembered, suddenly, that she had forgotten to make a definite appointment and state a meeting place. Her heart stopped, and she grew sick with sudden grief. He would never come back to her out of the mountains, and that one interview would be both the first and the last of him. She beat her fists together in a childish tantrum. She felt as a child, indeed, would have felt, had a fairy appeared before it, ready to answer any wish, and she had been too tongue-tied to question.

Her first impulse was to tell her father at once and let his men hunt down the fugitive, and yet she could not do that—partly because her word was pledged, and partly, also, because she felt assured that a hot pursuit might make the wanderer uncomfortable, indeed, but that it never could run him to the ground. The trail puzzles, as he had said, which could trouble a keen-scented grizzly would certainly be weird enough to baffle the strongest hunters who rode the range.

Now, as she stared before her, the shadow slid up onto the brow of a western hill. So soon had the runner passed across the valley that he must have run up the farther slope as easily and swiftly as he had run down that at her feet. His silhouette showed distinctly against the moonlit sky, and she made out the lump behind his shoulders which must be his pack; and the moonshine winked along the barrel of the rifle which he slung lightly in his hand as he ran. Then he was down out of sight in the winking of an eye. How empty and aching was the heart of the girl, seeing him go!

Chapter Nine

"The Ferret" Talks

Steffan's place had at one time been famous for the number of glasses which had rattled upon its bar, and though the country had gone dry, it was still strange to note the numbers of old and new patrons who still flocked to Steffan's as though drawn by the magic of its name. Along that bar they ranged, and with solemn faces sipped the ridiculous sodas and "pops" which now took the place of the good old throat-tearing, stomach destroying red-eye. Of course there was an explanation of the mystery, and a very crude one.

Worthy Mr. Steffan had simply brought in sundry barrels of moonshine which he kept in a shed behind his saloon. The barrels were on the edge of the floor of the shed, supported with wedges, and once these wedges were knocked away, the barrels would crash through the back of the shed and then pitch into vacancy down the long fall of the precipice, until they thundered into the little river far below.

An armed guard stood over those precious barrels night and day to shoot up any thirsty spirits who attempted to steal the good stuff, and to evade any sheriff's man by sending the loot shooting into the depths below. Twice the wily sheriff had tried to put his hands on the stock, and twice he had failed, and the whole quantity had gone to waste in the gorge beneath, to the misery of a thousand dry throats in the vicinity.

But Steffan himself controlled his grief. He merely doubled his prices and brought in fresh moonshine, raw and terrible with naked alcohol. Thus equipped, he furnished each glass of "soft stuff" that crossed his bar with a copious "stick" strong enough for the strongest old toper to lean upon. Business became more prospering with Steffan than ever before. He built a new wing to his house, increased his bar in size, put in a game room to the back of it, and established himself as a rising member of the community where he was more freely received than ever. He enjoyed a kind of popularity.

Such was Steffan's, where on this day a worthy cow-puncher by the name of "Mug" Doran resorted. His appearance was hardly more beautiful than his name. He was not thirty, but a premature baldness exposed the cramped and brutal slope of his forehead behind his brows, which were great projecting rings of bone. He was possessed, beneath this disappearing forehead, of a pair of little pale-green eyes, placed as close together as possible on either side of a still tinier nose, which had at one time tilted heavenward at the point, but which had been long since beaten flat by heavy fists in many and many a fight. His cheek bones, his mouth, and his chin, were the important features of his face. The cheek bones were like jutting rocks; his mouth was a wide and leathery slit; his chin had been battered many a time before, and would be battered many a time again, but it was still thrust dauntlessly forth in a defiance of the world.

Mug walked with a waddling lack of grace upon two very short legs, and around his narrow hips a gun was belted, but it was plain that the Colt was a concession to convention rather than an assistance to the gentleman. His real comfort and joy consisted in a pair of arms as huge in girth and in length as the legs were short and small. All of his movements were clumsy, but none so stiff as the turning of his head, which was placed upon a neck only two or three inches in length, apparently, and gorillalike in circumference.

Mug Doran walked to the bar and stood beside it, staring at the floor with his melancholy eyes, while the barkeeper rallied him in vain upon his downcast air and strove to win him to talk. But The Mug would have none of it. Once or twice he lifted those pale-green eyes, but it was to stare vacantly out the window and not into the face of the bartender. When he drank, it was still without turning around, but with furtive sips—half a glassful at a sip.

Having in this fashion finished two tall glasses of "soda," he turned reluctantly from the bar and seated himself upon the front veranda. All of this time he had not spoken a word, and now he sat with his legs and his lower body thrust out into the white-hot sun. He enjoyed that heat so much, indeed, that when his cigarette was half rolled he paused and let it stay in his hand uncompleted while he soaked in that burning sunshine. Presently a rider heaved into view down the cañon road and pushed his jogging horse into a tired canter at the sight of the parlor of peace and moisture. He pulled up his mount in a mist of reddish-brown dust through which he now strode, with a breath of that stained fog hanging about behind his shoulders.

The Mug gave him a cool and unfriendly scrutiny, but the newcomer paid not the slightest heed to Doran. One might have suspected that so fine an appearing man would be ashamed to be found in converse with such an ape as

The Whispering Outlaw

Doran. For Jerry Monson was as fine a picture of manly beauty as one could wish to see, bland and blond and smiling, as strong as he was tall, and as tall as he was handsome. He gave not the slightest heed to The Mug, but just before he passed through the swinging door into the saloon, the three forefingers of his right hand flattened against the side of his overalls, and he thrust out his thumb at a sharp right angle.

Then he was gone, but The Mug remained staring for another moment as though he still saw the picture of that hand displayed. At length he rose, yawned, and stretched out his long arms, and made off for his horse. He untethered the animal and lifted himself into the saddle with his long arms, instead of jumping, as others would do. Once in the saddle he rode off at a good round pace until he reached a point where the trail veered sharply to the right: The Mug rode straight ahead over a litter of rocks, and so down a short gulley between two mountainsides.

It was a lofty pass. On either side the rugged trees were climbing in smaller and in thinner ranks toward the timber line which was not far above their heads, and above that point the mossy sides of the mountains rolled into the sky, sometimes quite naked, sometimes covered with the dim flowers of the high bee pastures in delicate and pastel shades. The Mug gave these visions of delight a cursory glance, then touched his weary horse so deeply with

the spurs that he brought out a dot of crimson
upon either flank and sent him snorting and
racing around the side of the pass until he
drew up with braced feet, sliding to a halt over
the gravel.

Mug Doran now dismounted with sudden
nonchalance and waved a greeting to some
three or four men who were assembled around
or in a little shack near by. Foremost of these,
and now seated behind a little table in the shack,
was no less a personage than Lew Borgen. He
greeted Mug with a grunt; received a grunt in
ample payment for that courtesy, and dropped
his head to continue his meditations. Those
thoughts were not altogether pleasant, as could
be seen in his clouded and moody eye, fixed
upon the floor. Plainly Lew Borgen was worried, and indeed there were many new lines of
thought in his face since he had last been seen.
One might have said that he had paid amply
for the prosperity which had come to him, and
that rapidly growing bank account in a certain
Eastern town.

He waited here behind the old table until the
party had grown to its full size. When complete,
there were besides himself, Jerry Monson, and
Mug Doran, six others, who were, by name, Joe
Montague, Sam Champion, Nick Oliver, "Silver" Lambert, "Lefty" Anson, and finally Pete
Nooney. Pete arrived last of all on a sweating
roan with his whistle, as usual, running gayly
before him to announce that he was coming.

The Whispering Outlaw

Even the gloomiest among that nest of rascals could not help at least a semblance of a smile when that whistle of Pete's was heard dimly in the distance.

Finally they were assembled in a closed knot around the table, or sprawling upon the floor. The evening had commenced, and a roaring fire had been built in the fireplace, so that the room, as the daylight faded, was filled with a broken and dancing illumination. Sometimes it washed a wave of shadow over a man; sometimes it painted all his face in red; sometimes teeth glistened where someone yawned in a corner; sometimes sharp, wicked eyes burned out of a shadow.

Such was the assemblage. When they were all met and in order, Lew Borgen finally rose and said: "Gents, I guess, take it by and large, I ain't exactly welcome in here. But I heard tell that there was going to be a meeting of everybody else but me, and I sort of didn't like it. So I come along. But if I still ain't wanted, I hope that somebody will stand up and tell me why. I'm sure right here, open to reason, and just plumb waiting to be talked to."

It was a speech which could almost have been called humble, at least by those who were familiar with the violence which was natural to the big man. But there followed this demand, or rather appeal, an interval of silence in which no man looked at his fellows lest something should be seen in his eyes which might incline to point out the ringleader. There was no need of such a betrayal, however. From the farthest corner there stood up that man among them all who was the least in stature and the most terrible in fight.

It was Sam Champion, little, lithe, black eyed, black haired, with the glance and the pointed face of a ferret, and the incredible tenacity and ferocity of that little destroyer. A ferret will run across the very boots of a man when it is on a blood trail. It was known that Sam Champion had actually thrown himself into the hands of the law in order that he might destroy an enemy of his. He had neither scruples nor fear. There was no good in him, and there was no pretense of good. He existed in the world for the sake of the fights which he might be able to find in it.

To this small and terrible figure Lew Borgen turned with a faint shudder.

"Well, Sam?" he said.

"I'm the gent that spread the word around," said Sam.

He paused, with his wicked little eyes burning and snapping. "The reason why I didn't ask you here, Lew——"

"Ah," said Borgen, "that's what I want to hear."

"Well, it ain't going to please you none when you know it. The reason why I didn't ask you in on this here party was because I figured that you wouldn't be none too pleased to find out that we're meeting here tonight to find out who in the devil The Whisperer is!"

Indeed, it caused Borgen's head to shake in violent disapproval. "Sam, old son," he said, "I can't let you go no further. For your own sakes I can't let you go no further. It's the one thing that The Whisperer has always told me—the boys was never to meet up together except for business, and then only when they was called on by him to meet. When they did get together, I was never to let 'em talk about him."

"Here's the best part of a dozen of us," said Sam Champion with a touch of scorn. "Are we all going to be afraid of saying what we please about any one man?"

"I've heard gents talk like that before. What happened to 'em?"

"Who did you hear?"

"You know. I recollect telling you myself. That was when I seen that you was first getting restive. I come to you and told you my idea of what had happened to Tirrit. I told you my idea was that Tirrit got his because he started trying to get onto the trail of The Whisperer. Tirrit had been buzzing around asking me a lot of questions. I warned him that he was walking around on mighty dangerous ground. But the fool wouldn't be convinced. He wanted to find out for himself. And my idea is that the gent that shot down Tirrit was The Whisperer himself!"

It caused a stir of wonder in the little company.

"I'm talking about things I hadn't ought to talk about," said Borgen, in a very apparent anxiety. "God knows which one of you gents is acting as The Whisperer's spy on the rest of us."

"Maybe," cut in Sam Champion, "one of 'em is The Whisperer himself!"

Chapter Ten

Borgen Accused

This suggestion caused another general start, together with a play, and then a counterplay, of glances, but nothing could be arrived at in the way of a suspicion.

"No!" said Lew Borgen with the calm of perfect conviction. "I'll tell you open and free that there ain't a man here that's The Whisperer."

"You know that?" asked Sam Champion.

"Yep. I know that well enough."

"How come you to be so sure?"

"There's something about The Whisperer—if you was to see him, you'd know what I mean. I've never seen him by daylight. I've never seen him without a mask. But for one thing he's got a queer build—like a wedge; for another thing, there's a sort of hell-fire strength about him that paralyzes a man."

"Hold on, Lew. Don't talk foolish!"

Lew Borgen turned upon Champion. "Look here, Champion," he said, "if you've come here aiming to make trouble for me and work up a gun play so's you can have the fun of another fight on your hands, you've hunted up the wrong tree. I know you, Champion. I know you're fast with a gun and sure with a gun. Well, I know that I'm not so fast and not so sure as you are, and I don't aim to get murdered. Sooner than fight you, I'll tell the boys to take your guns away and throw you outside. And if you make any trouble after that, I'll have 'em kill you like a dog and leave you where you lie. There's more than one that maybe wouldn't lose no sleep about shoving a few chunks of lead inside of your ribs!"

This direct and terrible threat brought a sort of a groan of rage from the smaller man. He shook from head to foot with his passion, and his right hand clasped and unclasped the handle of his Colt. But he did not jerk the weapon out at once. Instead, he first looked around him upon the faces of his companions, and he saw there enough to make him pause for further thought.

They were looking upon him coldly, steadily, and they were one and all watching his gun hand.

The Whispering Outlaw

He knew what that meant, and he was touched with awe, for though he might have taken a chance with lesser men, with such fellows as these it would have been madness to court a fight. He was superior to any one of them, but only by a small margin, and any two of them would completely overmatch him. He brought his hand away from the weapon.

Lew Borgen was continuing the oration which he had begun with such a happy effect.

"You been always a trouble maker," he told "The Ferret." "Nothing is good enough for you so long as there's the chance for a fight somewhere near. Oh, I know you, Sam. I know where you were a few months back when I first met up with The Whisperer and started on this game. You was down and out. You'd done so much shooting and knifing that nobody would throw in to go partners with you. Then I come along and talked plain to you: 'Sam,' says I, 'you're down and out. You know why, and I know why. There ain't no mystery about it. You're too hard even for your friends. Well, Sam, I've got a chance to give you, because I know that you're as good a gun fighter as ever lived, and because you don't know what fear is!' I told you that, and then I told you what I told all the other boys, and you sure were happy to come in.

"You was down and out then, the same as some of the rest. Nick Oliver was flat. So was

Pete Nooney and Joe Montague, and I was flat busted myself except for the little pocket money that The Whisperer had give to me. Then what happened? You boys done what The Whisperer wanted you to do. There was a plan laid. Who pulled off the first job? Who cracked the first safe? The Whisperer did it all himself to show you boys that he knew his work and that he could make his living all by himself if he had to. What did he do then? He split up with you all. Gave you all your right share. More'n that, when Silver, there, and Pete and Mug Doran blew in all they'd made gambling, he staked them all over again, bought them hosses, and left them flush and prime.

"Ain't he gone right on? There ain't one of you has gone hungry. There ain't one of you that hasn't got money in his pocket right now. There ain't one of you that couldn't save up a mighty pretty piece of coin and put it away if he had as much as a mind to do it. These here things are all the straight stuff. Then you come along and try to corner The Whisperer and call him for a crook. Is it square, Sam? Is it square, boys?"

Whatever the glowering Sam might think, it was plain that the rest of the boys had no sympathy with him at that moment. With a hearty and even a ringing chorus they announced they were well pleased with what they had secured out of their silent partnership with the unknown criminal, and they would be only too delighted to see the concern of Mr. Whisperer and Co. continued ad infinitum. So Sam Champion looked gloomily around him, not knowing exactly what he should do next. However, he had not by any means discharged the last arrow in his quiver, and he now put another upon the string.

"Lew," he said to the lieutenant of The Whisperer, "who has seen The Whisperer outside of you?"

"Nobody."

"Who has heard him talk?"

"Nobody but me."

"Who knows whether he's young or old?"

"I ain't so sure of that myself."

"Who's got any idea of what he looks like?"

"I've told you boys what little I've seen—that he's uncommon broad in the shoulders and that he's got red hair and that he's just average height. That's all I can tell you. I've told it a pile of times."

"Boys," said Sam Champion to the others, and he deliberately turned his back upon Lew Borgen, "ain't it a queer thing that The Whisperer should keep himself in hiding like this?"

"I've told you why he says that he does it," muttered Borgen.

Sam held up his hand to indicate that he must not be interrupted before he had spoken his mind.

"Because he don't trust partners, is what Borgen tells us. But he has trusted Borgen, and it looks like the rest of us are worth trusting as much as Borgen. We've proved ourselves, I should say! Ain't it sort of strange that The Whisperer ain't showed himself to us to even hear how much we think of him? Ain't it queer that he don't come down, after all these months, just to say hello?"

The others admitted by their silence that they considered it rather odd.

"But," said Sam Champion, "it looks to me like it was a sort of fortunate thing for someone. That one is Borgen, there. Every time we turn a trick, Borgen gets two shares delivered to him for himself. That's sort of fat, but we don't grudge it. And then he gets three more shares for The Whisperer—delivered to himself!"

He paused to let this sink in. Then he added hastily: "And supposing—just supposing—that Borgen was The Whisperer himself—wouldn't it be sort of handy to get them five shares?"

It was a blow the more stunning because it was something which had, of course, occurred to every one of them. A sudden gust of wind took hold of the door of the shack like a hand and slammed it shut. It made every man jump and look about him with great eyes.

Then they turned to Borgen to see what he was to say. But Borgen, for the instant, was tongue-tied. This suggestion struck the nearer home to him because he had actually contemplated just such a practice. To be accused of a crime which he had attempted, paralyzed his tongue, and his face grew white as he confronted those prying eyes. When he realized that this pallor was betraying him, he grew yet more pale. He tried to smile. But his lips were numbed, and when he moistened them with the tip of his tongue, they trembled. Perspiration began to pour out upon his forehead.

"Gents," he said feebly, "this is a queer lay for me. D'you stand with Sam on this?"

A deadly silence greeted his appeal. Then he saw that they were scowling, and each man was leaning forward to read his face.

"Look here," broke in The Mug suddenly, as a thought struck him, "ain't it sort of queer that Borgen ain't never had a hand in any of the hard work of pulling off deals since them first two that he says was done by The Whisperer's lone hand? Whoever has to work, it ain't Borgen. He lies low and collects the double share he bargained for—and the three other shares, as Sam has just been saying. Sam, I'm mighty glad that you called this here meeting, and come to think about it, I'm mighty glad that Borgen is right here to hear us talk!"

There was another pause while this suggestion was digested.

Then another speaker cleared his throat. It was Anson, big, lumbering, rawboned, and a practical worker in the field of crime with few rivals. He had spent, altogether, some ten years in penitentiaries, but his nerve had not been broken. It had turned a great, impulsive giant into a fox, and that was all.

"Speaking of queer lays," he said, "I aim to say that the one I got last night was a rare beauty! I was told to take the best hoss I could lay my hands on and stand him under the trees near the house of the new sheriff, that swine of a Kenworthy. That was all I was told. I was told by Borgen that when the time come for me to do something, I'd know it without asking any questions. Well, the time comes! There's a noise in the house, and then about fifty of 'em boils out like hornets. They see me, and they pretty near ride me to death down the valley when I run for it. Borgen, I know you've had a grudge agin' me these three years. Was you trying to work it out on me that way? Was you trying to turn me over to 'em?"

"Borgen," put in Champion, "we got a case agin' you. You show us The Whisperer—or else——"

There was no need of filling in the threat. Borgen groaned, so great was his agony of mind.

"Boys," he said, "I leave it to you; I been pretty lucky in my way, but do you figure, any of you, that I got the *brains* to map out what The Whisperer has done? Another thing: Champion, you're hunting a bad trail when you try to locate The Whisperer. That was how Tirrit come to his end!"

"By heavens," cried Champion, "did *you* have

a hand in the killing of Tirrit? Was it you that finished my pal?"

He gripped his gun and glared at the big man.

Chapter Eleven

Champion's Fate

There was no question of appealing to allies against Sam Champion now. It was only a matter of how the lieutenant to The Whisperer could avoid an open conflict, for such a battle, he knew, could end in only one way—his own death. He himself was no stupid marksman, but he lacked that explosive nerve force which is typical of the expert gun fighter; he might be only a twentieth part of a second slower than Sam Champion in getting out his Colt, but that small fraction was as good as all eternity, for Sam would not have to pull his trigger more than once.

The others in the band sat or stood about like

lean-sided wolves, waiting, and eager only to see the fight, regardless of its outcome, favoring Sam Champion if they favored any one.

"Come out with it!" snarlingly exclaimed Champion. "It was *you* that bumped off poor Tirrit. You plugged him from behind!"

Sometimes a very great peril will actually shock all fear out of the breast of an endangered man. So it was now with Lew Borgen. His mind became perfectly clear as he prepared to fight for his life, with words, before he fell back upon his gun.

"Tirrit was shot from the front. You must remember that," he said dryly.

"He's boasting of it, boys! He's boasting that he shot down Tirrit!"

"Look here, Sam," said Borgen, more coolly than ever. "If you're crowding me for a fight, you'll get what you're after. Even if I ain't got one chance in ten to throw a gun as fast as you, I'll take no water, Sam. But about Tirrit—good heavens, boys, you all know what Tirrit was— he was faster than anybody among us with a gun, excepting Sam Champion, and maybe Joe Montague, yonder.

"Tirrit was a flash with a gun. I knowed it as well as the rest of you. He didn't like me, and I didn't like him. I admit that quick and easy, and there ain't no argument. But that's only one part of the proof that I killed Tirrit. I might have stood Tirrit off with a rifle at long distance, but I would of been a fool to go hunting him with a Colt. No, sir, you all know, if you steady down and take a think about it, that it was a better shot than me that killed Tirrit!"

He spoke this with such a quiet assurance that even the malignity of Sam Champion was shaken for an instant, and his hand dropped from his gun.

"But maybe some of you don't know," went on Borgen, "that Tirrit was hot on the trail of The Whisperer. Once, just before he finished, he come to me and says: 'Borgen, I used to think that you was The Whisperer. But now I've changed my mind. I've tracked you along through the mountains and seen you meet up with another hossman. Then I've tried to ride down the back trail of that other gent, but doggone me if I have any luck.'

"I says to him: 'Tirrit, leave off that trail of The Whisperer. He sure hates to be followed. Follow me as much as you want to, but don't follow me to try to get at who and what The Whisperer is!'"

"The devil!" broke in Champion in sardonic disgust.

"That's what Tirrit said," remarked Borgen. "Three days later, Tirrit lay dead."

"If I'd been there——" began Champion.

"You'd of gone the same way," said Borgen.

"You lie!"

"Champion, you can't talk like that to me."

"I ain't started to talk to you, Borgen. I ain't

started to tell you all the kinds of a skunk that I know you to be!"

There was no avoiding a fight now. They were tense with it; and the savages who encircled them, looked on with lips grinning in wolfish satisfaction at the combat which was to follow. They did not shrink back from the probable line of fire. For a gun even in the dying hand of such an expert as either of these, could not fail to shoot straight. They stood close, and they waited, shifting their eyes greedily from one face to the other to read, if they might, the fierceness or the dread which was showing in either of the combatants.

They saw Champion shivering like a ferret with eagerness for the battle. They saw Borgen white, hopeless, but determined. Though he was no better than a dead man, they felt, they could not but admire him as they observed his bearing and his manner. Death, then, hung not a second away from someone in that little shack, and now Champion delivered his final blow.

"Now that you've robbed the sheriff's house and gutted his safe, how'll we know how much money there was in it? How'll we know whether or not you're cheating us on the split, eh?"

It was the final insult. But before Borgen could act upon it and draw, a draught of air passed through the shack like a human sigh. The two combatants dared not take their eyes from each other, though they knew that the door of the house had swung open. But presently they heard someone murmur an exclamation, and they swung about of one accord, and they saw in the open doorway a man of middle height with extraordinarily broad shoulders, so that his build was wedge-like to the extreme. He wore a sombrero with a great limp brim that slid down half across his eyes, yet beneath this brim they caught sight of one or two rusty red curls of hair. His face and even the back of his head was obscured by a black mask. For the rest, his appearance was that of any cow-puncher in overalls and leather chaps. Altogether, in fact, his costume was most simple and workmanlike.

"Champion," said this apparition in a whisper, or in a murmur even less piercing than a whisper, "Champion, you rat, get out your gun!"

Champion, with a groan of dread, his teeth showing like a cornered rat indeed, went for his Colt. But he suddenly spun around with a scream and pitched forward upon his face, for the masked stranger had beaten him on the draw.

The Ferret lay without stirring. The stranger tossed into the room a thick wallet, which struck upon the back of the fallen man, unfolded, and exposed, inside, two thick sheafs of greenbacks. While the glances of the gang turned to this, The Whisperer disappeared; for when they looked up again, he was gone from before the door.

Neither did any of them care to follow his trail or to make further inquiries into his existence.

Lew Borgen, who had seen him before, and now had been delivered from the extremest danger by his last appearance, seemed hardly less shocked than any of the others in the gang by what had happened. He took up the big wallet, and there was nothing said while they turned the body of Sam Champion upon his back and saw that he had been shot fairly between the eyes, as though the man, or devil in the form of a man, who had just been before them, had chosen to exhibit his skill.

"Here's something from The Whisperer," said Lew Borgen, bringing a piece of paper out of the wallet, and he showed to them a white scrap upon which a brief message had been hastily printed.

"Let the boys split up this loot in the regular way," he read to them. "Except that Anson gets his own share and my three shares. I had my part out of the game. I think the sheriff will agree."

This was signed, the name being printed neatly like the rest of it.

It was an amazing letter to receive, and it could not have come more opportunely. The gang watched the lieutenant count out the spoils. There was the considerable sum of twenty-five thousand dollars, and every dollar was made ten-fold sweet by the understanding that it had come from the house and the safe of the sheriff, himself, on the very evening when he had been feasting his friends and boasting that The Whisperer and his gang were put down forever.

The division was made on the spur of the moment. With their hands full of money, the dead man upon the floor was almost forgotten. They carried him out at last and placed his body in a rift among the rocks. Then they climbed upon either side of the little gully above him and pried loose and rolled down upon him a monumental mass of tons of rock. This was his burial, and when it was completed, the cavalcade turned soberly away. They had their pockets full of money, to be sure, but they were very thoughtful. Two men fell back behind the others and entered into a most serious conversation.

They were Joe Montague and Jerry Monson. They drew their horses back to a slow walk and so let the rest drift farther ahead of them; neither did they talk to each other, but scowled at the road, as though even through the silence their grave thoughts were being communicated to each other.

Finally Joe Montague broke the quiet. "How does it look to you, Jerry?" he asked.

"The same way it looks to you, old son—spooky as the devil, I'd call it!"

Joe shuddered, and they fell silent again, scowling more than ever.

"At least," said Jerry, "that ghost has treated the boys pretty square."

"Has it?"

"What you mean by talking in that tone?"

"A few weeks back there was four of us—there was you and me and Tirrit and Sam Champion. We'd all swore to hang close together, and we'd hung close together just the way we swore we would. We'd gone into all the same things together. We'd fought for each other. We'd pulled each other out of the hole many a time, eh, lad? And now, all in a few weeks, half of us are gone!"

"You mean that The Whisperer has it in for us?"

"I don't mean nothing," muttered the other, glancing nervously behind him as though he feared even then that the dreadful figure which had destroyed Champion a short time before might be hovering upon wings to overhear this conversation. "I don't mean nothing, but I'll tell you plain and fair, speaking man to man, that I got a feeling in my bones that you and me, old son, are due to get bumped off next. You can lay to that!"

Upon this cheerful disclosure they both meditated for a considerable space. When a landslide suddenly rumbled in the far distance they both started and then cursed.

"Jerry," said Joe Montague at length, "who could The Whisperer be—if you think he's got it in for us, the same as I think?"

"I dunno," answered Jerry. "The four of us have stepped on a good many toes, in our day."

"We have."

"But ain't there been a good reason for Tirrit and Champion to have been bumped off? They was each of 'em trying to get something on The Whisperer."

"That's something *I'll* never try."

"Nor me."

"D'you think we'd better make a run for it?"

"No, I say, stay by the guns and keep watching and waiting. If The Whisperer is after us, running away ain't going to help none!"

"That's a true thing."

They plodded on. Once Jerry thought he heard a crunching of gravel behind them as of an approaching horse, and he crowded close to Joe, cursing with fear. Once they both reined in their horses with one accord, as though they saw, at the same instant, a form in the night in front of them.

Chapter Twelve

Kenworthy's Move

Kenworthy was a man whose level temper and genial good nature, even under trying conditions, were universally admired, but it must be admitted that he passed under a cloud after the invasion of his house and the blowing of his safe. He would not believe that there existed in the world a man at once so bold and so foolish as to recklessly defy him, Percival Kenworthy, formidable not only in himself, but now made doubly awful by his office of sheriff.

He spent a solid week melting horseflesh upon the mountain trails and contributing even a quantity of his own none too solid weight. Then he came back to his ranch house looking a little more tanned than usual, with his face a trifle thinner. But he was at least able to smile again, and, holding up his head, he could present a fair face to the world after what he considered his shame.

Considerable time was spent in planning what rôle would be the best for him to assume, but finally he decided there was much to be said if only he could open his lips. He went into town, therefore, wearing a smile which did not come off even when the most eminent of the citizens saw him and went to make more special personal inquiry of what he had seen and done on the trail of the famous criminal. To their questions, Kenworthy replied with a smile and a wave of the hand. It was as much as to say that everything was getting on very well, and that before long he would have news for them that would be surprising. With this they had to be content, while the sheriff went on to his office, where he sat swearing at the blank wall before him and grinding his teeth and praying for an inspiration.

It was not the loss of the money which so greatly affected him. It was the loss of his prestige. He was known as the man who never failed; and he would have thrown another fifty thousand dollars after twenty-five which he had already lost if he could have lodged The Whisperer safely behind the bars of a prison or seen him lying dead at his feet.

The Whispering Outlaw

He was not foolish enough to trust to his own unaided efforts, however. For Percival Kenworthy was one of those rare men who are convinced of their superiority to all others and who yet, in their heart of hearts well understand that they have only succeeded in the world because of favorable position, money, inherited influence, and the hired brains of others thrown into their affairs. Of his own weakness Kenworthy was not unaware, though he found an excuse for it, or at least a high attitude from which to regard it.

Many a king, he told himself, did everything through ministers and the generals, and yet the ministers and the generals were forgotten, and, in the annals of history, the name of the king alone was remembered. What he decided was that he would hereafter show his hand less and less. Instead, he would rely more and more upon experts and specialists. He now wanted to capture a man. He himself could not even capture a cow.

He had become a great and famous rancher without ever learning to swing a rope or shoot straight with a revolver, but he had hundreds in his employ who could do both things. He was a fool, then, to suddenly appear like a knight at the head of forces and ride out through the mountains. He could only make himself saddle weary and render himself less magnificent in the eyes of other and lesser men.

That very day two men arrived in response to telegrams which he had dispatched immediately after the robbery in his own house. He had hoped that when they arrived he would have finished the business, and could dismiss them with a grand gesture. But now it appeared that he was too sadly in need of them.

They called at his office the same day that he reached town after his return from the trail of The Whisperer. The first to come in was a tall man, built narrowly from head to foot. Only his feet and his hands were huge. The rest of him looked like a normal man who had been taken by the top and bottom and stretched out half a dozen inches longer than he was meant to be. He was about two inches over six feet, and he weighed less than a hundred and fifty pounds! He had a head like a parrot's, being very small, very round, with a great red beak of a hooked nose, and two tiny and extraordinarily bright eyes set close in on either side of the nose. He had protruding teeth of great length from which his lips fell away in a continual smile. In short, he was exactly the sort of a gawky man at whom the little boys in the street love to point their fingers. Even Percival Kenworthy, though he knew the importance of his caller, had to blink twice or thrice before he could readjust his thoughts with what his eyes told him.

He had before him the celebrated "Stew" Morrison, more formally known as Oliver

Wainwright Morrison, and hence also nicknamed "Ow" Morrison. He was a man of fifty who looked forty; he was a ridiculous mask of ugliness and femininity, and yet he had the heart of a hero; he looked like a simpleton who should have been sheltered carefully from the roughness of the world, and yet he had been for fifteen years one who earned his living by following the man trail.

Stew Morrison folded his immense brown hands around one knee and watched with lackluster eyes while his patron detailed the difficulties of the job. When Kenworthy ended he asked abruptly what Mr. Morrison would charge, and Mr. Morrison assured him that he never worried about charges until he felt himself really on the trail, and that on this occasion, if he captured The Whisperer, he felt that Mr. Kenworthy would probably give him more than he, himself, had the effrontery to ask.

With this assertion he withdrew, promising that he would begin work at once. He stepped out on the street, whistling to his heels at a little, yellow-hided cur which skulked along with its tail between its legs and its nose so close to its master's feet that it had to halt at each step as the heels of the man hunter rose. The sheriff had gone to the window to watch the tall and gawky form stride down the street, and now he flushed with shame and laughed with amusement as he followed this specter with his glance. He would rather lose ten thousand, he decided, than have the public at large know that he had hired such a creature as a confidential agent.

He had hardly reseated himself in front of his desk when his second caller arrived. This was a man as far opposed in appearance to Old Morrison as it was possible to imagine. He was a broad and burly chunk of a man with a businesslike eye, and an immense energy showing in all of his movements. When he sat down and clapped his hands upon his knees and looked at the sheriff, the glance from his eyes was like the thrust of another's hands, and strong hands at that. He heard the details from beginning to end, and then he spoke.

"I've read up the whole thing," said Mr. Stephen Rankin. "I think I know this case backward already. I've already thought of a clue that nobody else has noticed. I've already thought of a criminal though nobody else has even looked that way."

Mr. Kenworthy was delighted by such a bearing of brisk decisiveness, and he could hardly refrain from saying so, though it was his policy never to praise men with words; but to let his money speak for him in that respect after he had been served.

"I have my own suspicion," he said, "that there may be some rascal in my own house who has betrayed me, working in conjunction with someone on the outside, of course. There's a great deal pointing in that direction. Who but a servant would have known where the safe was, or how to move so smoothly into and out from the house?"

The second man hunter swallowed a smile and made himself look gravely into the face of the sheriff.

"I see," he said, "that you have had a great deal of experience in our profession——"

"You might call me a novice; I have only begun," said the sheriff, as happy as a girl at the prospect of a compliment.

"Well," said Mr. Rankin, "it's a hard life, but it might amuse you. In the meantime, I'll follow up your clue along with some of my own."

"And your rate?"

"My rate, sir, is like a doctor's. It goes up and down with the nature of the service and the size of the patient's income. In your case—why, I think that ten thousand dollars might be——"

"Ten thousand hell cats!" shouted the rancher.

"Dollars," said the detective, and smiled calmly upon him. "Sometimes I mend reputations, and sometimes I *make* 'em!"

Chapter Thirteen

Mr. Glenhollen

The worthy sheriff was himself amazed when, ten minutes later, Mr. Rankin walked out of the office with all of his terms agreed to; he was to have ten thousand dollars in cash, payable the instant the criminal was placed in the hands of the sheriff. Moreover, he agreed to disappear as soon as he had done his work, take no portion of the public eye or the public credit for his work, and let all the honor, if possible, rest upon the shoulders of Mr. Kenworthy.

This part of the contract was infinitely sooth-ing to the sheriff, but even so, he found that the prospect of paying out ten thousand dollars, in addition to his other losses was a hornet's sting indeed! He strove to be philosophical, however, and told himself that there was only one thing of true worth in life, and that this was reputation, as the poet proclaimed; his own repute had been damaged, and how lucky was he if the expenditure of money could restore his tarnishing fame!

For men everywhere were beginning to smile at a sheriff who could not protect his own house from the invasion of the criminal against whom he had arrayed all the forces of the law. He felt that he had this day added two strings to his bow. The one, Stew Morrison, might be of very small service, but the other was a man upon whom he felt he could reasonably build. Besides, the best things demand the best prices, and the hardest nuts have the sweetest kernels.

He had just fortified himself with that maxim when fate presented him with a more delightful consolation, one which quite wiped from his mind, by its importance, all thought of The Whisperer and his fellow malefactors. For there now appeared at the door of his office no other person than young Alexander Glenhollen, the son of the only rancher in the mountains who could lay a claim to greater acres and more coin in the bank than Mr. Kenworthy himself. His fortune was perhaps less widely known, because Mr. Alexander Glenhollen, senior, was a man who did not talk, even at his own board, and so the world remained in ignorance of his wealth, to some extent.

But the well-informed bankers, including Mr. Kenworthy, knew that Mr. Glenhollen's fortune had mounted up into the millions, and that under his wise management it was increasing each year. Mr. Kenworthy himself knew that he could drop all of his estate within that of the Glenhollen fortune and that there would be still room enough left for his to rattle about from side to side.

His eyes, therefore, widened a little as he rose to greet young Mr. Glenhollen. On the whole, he sincerely disliked young men, because he held that the salt and the savor of life did not appear in a man until he was well past forty, at least; at fifty, say, they began to be truly mellow. Mr. Kenworthy was at this time exactly fifty. However, the voice and the handshake which Mr. Kenworthy now offered to Mr. Glenhollen were of that pattern which he ordinarily reserved for the widows of deceased directors in his bank.

Mr. Glenhollen sat down. He was a young man as erect as football and crew in a great university could make him. The muscles of his neck were so stiff and thick that he could not help carrying his head like a conquering hero. He had a tawny growth of hair which was often uncombable, which, when it stood on end, gave him the unmistakable look of a ruffian. He had a pair of blue eyes, pale, and full of fires which had long ago burned in a viking ancestor, who carved out his fortune upon the iron coast of Scotland. He had a jaw which seemed to invite buffets, but, above all, he had a smile which dawned suddenly and delightfully now and then and which proclaimed him a prince of good fellows.

He now placed his hands upon his knees in a way that reminded Mr. Kenworthy very much of the detective who had last sat in that same chair. But there were great differences between their manners. The detective had talked with the smoothest assurance. Mr. Glenhollen grew alternately crimson and white, and his voice disappeared in his stomach and then trembled in his nose. But at length he managed to tell the sheriff that he, Mr. Glenhollen, ventured to aspire toward the hand of his daughter, and that he wished to secure the permission of the father before he addressed his attentions to the child.

Mr. Kenworthy closed his eyes. He was almost fainting with bliss; he grew pale with it. When he thought of the tremendous significance of this alliance it occurred to him that the god of love was not blind after all, but was a most blessed little deity. His daughter married to young Glenhollen! He would not have ventured to have even hoped for such a thing; it was too perfect. But, in the meantime, his closed eyes and his pale face seemed to be misinterpreted by the prince. That wretched young man was stammering and fast being wrecked by confusion.

"Does Rose know anything of this?" asked the sheriff suddenly.

"No," said Glenhollen. "The fact is, sir, I have only seen her half a dozen times or so; of course she hadn't even noticed me. That's why I'm calling on you today, so that I'll have a chance either to make her notice me or else to find out that she doesn't care to be troubled—in fact, Mr. Kenworthy, I'm confoundedly out in these things. I've never looked at a girl twice before in my whole life. I have a sister, you know, and she's about all the women I knew. Sometimes she was a little too much," he added with his grin, and his forelock, which had been pasted into place, rose and flared in the draught from the open window.

"Well, sir?" he added, very pale and equally brusque. "What do you say? Is she engaged somewhere else?"

Mr. Kenworthy arose. He took one of the brawny brown hands of the young man between both of his pudgy ones.

"My boy, my boy," he said with a quivering voice, "this is one of the greatest days in my life. Go on and win her. There are no other engagements—certainly there are no others!"

They drove out to the ranch that afternoon. Mr. Kenworthy had forgotten all about The Whisperer. He had forgotten all about every other trouble in this world. He was deep in the rosy contemplation of millions. With the financial hand of the giant Glenhollen behind him, all of his schemes could be put into being and made fruitful at once.

He gave himself five years for the erection of a giant corporation whose power should be felt across the continent—across the world. He saw himself summoned to Manhattan; he met the godlike powers of the Street; they shook him by the hand and called him by his first name; he sat down with them, enshrined in shimmering mahogany and soundless rugs; he squeezed between his fingers a hand-made cigar of choice-selected leaf; they were silent—they leaned forward in their chairs—he told them of the West and its possibilities, what it could do for them, and what they could do for it.

He looked still further into the heart of this golden cloud. He saw his services recognized by his home community, and that home community was now all the great realm between the Rockies and the Sierras; he found his name inserted in the histories which the school children must study.

Here the equipage rolled into the view of the ranch, and he was dragged from the heart of his dream into acute consciousness of his companion and his conversation, which had been maintained steadily during the entire trip from the town. It had been of a nature which required only a monosyllable now and again, for young Mr. Glenhollen was deep in the description of how he had first met Rose Kenworthy, and of a mysterious rose-colored dress which she was wearing at the time, and of how, when she turned her head toward him, she had smiled, not at him, but toward him, and he had told himself that to have this smile given to him for his own sake would be more delightful than to own all the riches of the world.

That was not all. There were other anecdotes which followed. The low voice and the dreamy air of her father led him on. He talked to himself rather than to a listener. Indeed, he was unheard, and the rancher only awakened enough, now and again, to murmur to himself: "It is true; it is not a dream, the fish is still wriggling upon the hook! Oh, what a blessing is a daughter with a lovely face."

So they swung over the top of the hill and came in view of the ranch house. Northward, in a great semicircle, were the mountains, lifted to the region of eternal snows. From their knees the foothills rippled away toward the south, sliced with gorges, brilliant with silver streaks where the snow-fed streams raced away toward the southland. Kenworthy House was like a small town, so great was the surrounding and the supporting cluster of his barns, sheds, corrals, and outbuildings of half a dozen different kinds. His practiced eye could distinguish the roofs of the granaries, the blacksmith shop which was one of the prides of his heart, the big wagon sheds, one after the other, the barn set apart for the shelter of the milk cows—and on and on, like separate lines of an exquisite poem. His companion had stopped talking with a gasp.

"The boy has sense," said the sheriff, with a sigh of satisfaction. "He has sense enough to see that a silly girl is one thing, but that a ranch is another—it's a—a creation!"

He had never yet been able to find just the word for it. But he was sure that when God looked down upon the world, His eye lingered longest on one special spot.

But what young Glenhollen said was: "My God, Mr. Kenworthy, do you think that I'll have a chance to win her?"

The rancher breathed out his disappointment. After all, he decided that the boy was shallow, as all young fellows are shallow; he needed time to ripen him.

"A chance?" said he. "There is no question about that; I have made up my mind; at this instant you are as good as married to her!"

They encountered Rose in her best humor. She had been riding a new mount, a cow pony gifted by nature, or a reversion to ancient ancestry, with the slender, strong legs, and the noble head of a true Arab. That first ride had been like a first conversation with a new and delightful mind, and she came in from the stables with her color high in her brown cheeks and her eyes merry and kind. Young Glenhollen almost swooned with joy and with fear.

"Courage, man!" said the father kindly. "Alec, you shall have her—a neat trick of a girl, eh, my boy? But why are you backing into the wall? She'll not bite you, lad!"

Her manner to the prince royal was, in the eyes of her father, shockingly careless and full of a reckless bonhommie rather than a maidenly and blushing dignity. She came straight up to him, called him by his first name, shook him heartily by the hand, and then excused herself to go change for dinner, which came early on the ranch. The rancher looked after her with alarm and dismay; he was about to apologize for such tomboy carelessness when he observed that young Glenhollen had fallen into a foolish ecstasy; and that he was so moved that his unruly and stiff-standing forelock was trembling without the touch of any wind.

He conducted Glenhollen into the library to wait for dinner, but that young worthy was incapable of conversation.

"If he is going to play the ass," said the rancher to himself, "I shall have a time with Rose, confound him!"

Play the ass he did, acting during dinner in such a fashion that Rose cast half a dozen wondering looks at him and then at her father; for when young Glenhollen made a conversational break, her father came nobly to his assistance and carried him through the crisis. There was only one good feature in the evening, and this was that Glenhollen insisted on leaving shortly after dinner, but with a promise to return the next day.

Chapter Fourteen

In the Garden

What on earth!" cried Rose when she was alone with her father again. "What on earth have you done to poor Alec. He's been transformed from a darling to a blockhead!"

"Can you guess what's happened?" cried her father, trembling with joy as he spoke.

"You and Alec are mixed up in some sort of a business deal."

"Right, girl, right. Can you guess what sort of business? It's you, my dear. You're to marry Alec—the Glenhollen and Kenworthy fortunes rolled together shall be the pedestal on which I—er—mount to great——"

She listened to him first in horror, then in

amusement, then in consternation.

"But, dad," she broke in at last, "is this really not a joke?"

"Joke?" he thundered. "Joke? If there's a joke in this, I'll have the young puppy shot! No, there's no joke in it. I watched his face, and it was all there. He was delirious with love. He——"

"Poor Alec!" cried the girl.

"Poor? He's not to be pitied. How could he do better than marry my daughter? After my death, he gets the estate with you!"

"Dad, is this serious? Am I to be married to—to—a football player who never had a thought in his life?"

"Hell's fires!" exclaimed the father, who fell back upon this oath whenever he was moved. "Does a man who has ten millions at his disposal have to be able to think also?"

"I suppose," said Rose, "that he does not have to be loved, either."

"Certainly not," said her father. "Will you tell me, silly girl, that you cannot be enough interested in such a fortune to marry the master of it? Besides," he continued, warned to be cautious by a certain familiar light in the eye of his daughter, "you have never yet found a young fellow you could care for, my dear, and if you ever expect to marry, I imagine you had better marry out of friendship and let love take care of itself."

He saw that he had here struck a point that

moved her; for she began to frown thoughtfully, and he could have rubbed his hands with
satisfaction. She was twenty-two, but a girl at
22 is apt to consider herself well on in life;
and with all the impulsiveness of Rose there
was a touch of hard practical sense in her that
made her ponder the words of her father the
more deeply. It was true that she was beginning to think that she should never find love,
and certainly more than one successful marriage had been founded upon nothing more
than friendship.

"Take a walk in the garden," said her father
kindly, "and think it over. Alec has come to a
foolish age, I'm afraid. When a man takes it
into his head to marry, if he's foiled in one
direction he'll take the next easiest road, and
if you let him slip or stand him off with a bit
of hard treatment he's apt to throw his cap into
another ring."

So it was that Rose went into the garden
obediently. It was a bit of conventionalized
wilderness. A brawling mountain stream, drove
across the grounds of the ranch-house toward
the corrals, where it was piped into various
troughs and pools lined with stone flagging
and furnished the horses and cattle with the
purest of drinking water. It flowed past a corner of the house, and thence under a stone wall
which enclosed the garden, dipping out beneath
another arch on the farther side.

The garden was of some size, and the trees

had been allowed to stand as they were originally found, but the undergrowth had been cleared away and stretches of lawn were planted here and there. A partial dam served to back the water in one place into a long and twisting pond whose banks were covered with flowers and flowering shrubs; and the walks with which the garden was interspersed were allowed to wander here and there where the contours led them.

She followed the first one she came to and finally sat down on a bench with her back to a tree and her face to the pool and the mountains beyond it. The surface of the water was bright with the alpenglow, and the snowy summits beyond were now all delicate rose on the western sides and translucent purples to the east. So that the girl in half a minute had forgotten the problem which she had come here to solve. That alpenglow was beginning to fade when she became aware of someone standing behind her. She turned and looked up into the face of the man of the forest.

He was leaning against the broad trunk of the tree, his arms folded across his breast, and his glance fixed on the same picture which she had been watching. She started, not only in wonder, but a little guiltily at the sight of him, for the memory of that first meeting by night had grown more and more into a dreamlike texture, and this day she had come close to disclosing the adventure to her father.

"I've come for the rest of the questions," he told her, still looking at the northern mountains and not at her. "I suppose you have them all in order by this time."

"You promised to come to me within a day," she reminded him.

"I have been in great trouble," said the stranger soberly.

"I'm sorry for that."

"I found the honey," he said.

He held out to her, what she had not hitherto noticed, a little cone of twisted bark, the inner bark of the birch, almost as supple and tough as leather and snowy in whiteness. A flap of the same substance covered the top of this improvised cup, and, lifting the flap, he allowed her to look down into a mine of amber honey, glistening as if lighted from within.

"Is this for me?" she asked.

He nodded, and when she looked up to him sharply, quizzically, to make out what could be the meaning behind this gift, she found his face as immobile as ever. He had remembered her in mere friendship; this was no woodland courtship, to be sure; and she felt herself a little baffled and confused on account of her first suspicion.

"After I found the honey," he said, "I came back, and crossed the trail of Madame Grizzly, headed in the same direction. But the same day a batch of dogs and hunters came after her and cornered her. I went along with her to help out.

That was hard work, too. Dogs are a nuisance, you know; and while I was working for Bruin I had to keep out of sight of the hunters, which made it harder still."

She was on fire with excitement at this.

"You saved the poor creature!"

"It was a narrow squeeze. They ran her from the early morning until the evening, straight-away over the mountains nearly fifty miles. She had three rifle bullets in her, so that she left a trail of crimson, and when the blood stopped running, she was a bit weakened and began to grow stiff. She was ugly as an old Tartar, too, and if I came too close to her, she was apt to make a pass at me with her paws. One pass will knock a man into eternity, you know! I've seen a dead cow with her ribs torn out by one such pass!"

"The terrible old—fool!" cried the girl. "Hasn't she sense enough to know a friend?"

"It's a bit confusing to a brute mind," he explained. "When some men shoot at one and one man is friendly—it's rather hard for an eye which cannot recognize faces to make out the difference. If she had not been so excited, I suppose she would have been amiable enough. At any rate, in the evening they cornered her.

"She had taken a path up a cañon—Donnelly Gulch, you know, planning to go up the side of the cliff where the horses could not follow her after she had worked her way to the top of the pass. But when she got there, she found that luck was against her. A landslide had whisked down the side of the cliff and rolled away all the boulders she had planned to climb by. There was nothing left for a clawhold except the smooth face of the rock, and it was very steep. She tried it a couple of times and slid back to the bottom almost at once. Then she looked around for another way out, but she was securely bottled. Behind her the hunt was coming; and in front of her there was the smooth rock on the one hand and a gulch thirty feet wide on the other.

"She saw that she was done for unless a miracle happened, so she got up on her hind legs, gave a battle roar, and then started ambling down the pass to make her last stand, as a good bear ought to do. I looked around for something to do, and presently I found something which I thought might serve."

"Thank heavens!" cried the girl, clasping her hands together in her excitement.

"I whistled to bruin. It was a call I used to use when I found that the fish were biting fast in a pool, and that there would be a good fat remnant left after I had all that I needed for myself. She could hear that call for miles, it seemed. You know their ears are wonderfully sensitive. I've seen that old lady sit up and clap her paws over her ears when a landslide came thundering down into a valley where she happened to be."

"But how did you get her safely across the

gulch? That was the only way, I suppose?"

He smiled at her impatience.

"Yes. That was the only way. She came back to me, when she heard me whistle, and she sat up and looked me in the face as though she wondered what the devil I could possibly do to be of assistance."

"Poor thing!"

"I got out my hatchet and tackled a tree. It was a big fellow, half ripped across at the base, and already leaning toward the gulch. The lightning had sawed it half in two; it had rotted part way. But there was still enough sound rind to keep it nearly erect. I couldn't cut through what remained in hours with such a light tool as a hatchet. But I hoped that I might weaken it enough to make it fall of its own landing weight.

"In the meantime, that roar of the bear's seemed to have huddled the hunters together for a time. They whistled in their dogs and seemed to get ready for her rush. But when they found she did not come, they started up the ravine again and sent the dogs ahead. I could hear those big brutes yelling like devils as they came. I was working in uncomfortable quarters, too. I didn't know when my friend the grizzly would make a pass at me with one of those dangling forepaws of hers, and she was near enough to reach me with the nearest flip."

He paused again to indulge in one of those

silent laughs of his, and then his soft voice went on again. She was more fascinated than ever as she saw that he was not so much simply telling the narrative to her as he was rehearsing the tale for his own benefit, recalling the least incidents with delight like the joy of a child.

"I blazed away with my hatchet like a madman. The old tree began to groan; and at the same time a host of dogs came out of the trees on the rush; they bayed for their kill like good fellows, and then began to yell in a different note when they saw a man actually standing there in company with a hundred-per-cent grizzly. They couldn't make this out, while Madame sat back on her haunches and prepared to bat them into a future life with either hand if they came within reach. I sank the blade of the hatchet with all my might into the central cord of the rind of sound wood; and it was like cutting the cable that holds a ship.

"The whole top of the tree lurched down and made a sound like the rising of a great wind over our heads. It landed on a fir on the opposite edge of the gulch and smashed that tree into kindling wood as though it were a hollow match box. The stump had ripped in two, of course, and the big, rotten butt of the tree made a side jump at me. It missed me by an inch."

He paused to recall the shudder of that falling monster.

"There was our bridge, of course," he went on, "and Madame needed no explanation of why I had chopped the tree down. She ambled across the trunk of the tree and I ran along after her. But just as she got to the end of the trunk the old demon turned around, wrinkled her nose at me, and gave me a snarl that turned my blood to ice."

"Oh, ingratitude!"

"You see, she's not a bear in a fairy tale; she's a grizzly playing up to form. At any rate, I got out of sight before the men came up. Their dogs had scampered across the fallen stump. But they couldn't follow their dogs on foot and leave their horses behind them. Besides, it looked as though the dogs could never bring the old grizzly to bay. So they called off the dogs and went back. But first they gathered around the stump and examined it. They couldn't make out what had happened.

"There were the marks of my hatchet clearly enough to be seen, I imagine; and if they had looked very carefully at the ground, they could have made out places where I had stood, though I had taken a little care to step on stones. At any rate, they saw none of these things, and when they went home they carried with them the most wonderful bear story that was ever told— of how a grizzly actually bit and clawed in two the decaying stump of an old tree and so made a bridge for herself across to the other side of a gorge. They'll all swear to that, I know!"

"I think I've heard of some such thing," she told him. "But of course, even a bear story is nothing in these days of The Whisperer."

"What is that?"

"Do you mean, really, that you've never heard?"

He assured her that he had not, for only now and again rumors and murmurs came to him from the world of daylight and of men. Sometimes he stole up on a camp fire and listened to the talk around it; once he had been shot at for a prowling beast of prey on such an excursion; sometimes parties passed him, or single hunters, while he was hiding and sleeping in the woods by day; and so, out of random words here and there, he made up a few hints of what was happening in the world. It was hard news for her to digest, but he told it so simply that she found herself drawn in spite of herself to believe him.

Here a gate clanged, and a cow-puncher ran up through the garden toward the house, breaking a strict law to the effect that no one saving the family must pass through the garden; but he probably had something of importance to report. The girl looked to her strange visitor in terror lest he should be seen, but he had vanished into the thinnest air.

Chapter Fifteen

Paying the Penalty

The old chilly feeling of the unearthly which had come so strongly upon her at the first meeting with the man of the night had been dispelled, somewhat, on their second meeting, by his most daylight cheerfulness, and that pleasant tale of the delivery of the old bear from her hunters. Rose Kenworthy thought the story remarkable enough, but certainly there was nothing ghostly about it. Besides, the daylight had made it possible for her to see the unkempt length of his hair and the tattered condition of the deerskin in which he was chiefly dressed, and these calmly noted facts were surely far removed from the realm of mystery.

He became more singular and less terrible with every instant; and though a shock passed through her when she found that he had vanished, she could not help but smile when, a moment later, she discovered that he had simply fallen noiselessly to the ground where, however, he made no effort to flatten himself, but trusting to the height of the shrubs and the thickness of the evening to shield him, he rested his head upon his hand and, lying at ease there, addressed her in a measured and cautious voice.

She did not hear what he said, but watched the cow-puncher out of sight toward the house, and then she sighed as she looked back to the stranger.

"That was a narrow escape," she told him.

"No," he answered, "a man like that fellow sees nothing until it has been pointed out to him. A horse has been skinned up a bit in some barbed wire, and now he's running with his mouth open to tell the news to your father who will light another cigar and tell him that he never thinks about horses or any other part of the ranch after dinner."

She cried out beneath her breath; for it was exactly what her father would have said under such circumstances.

"How can you know him so?"

"I spent an evening watching him through the window of his library a few days ago. It was easy to read—his lips."

The Whispering Outlaw

She knew that he meant a "mind" instead of "lips," and she flushed a little; she wanted to say something in defense of her poor father, but then she controlled herself and wondered still more that this wild man should have made her feel apologetic for any member of her own family. Yet how clear it was that at a glance he had pierced to the fatuous heart of the rich rancher! How had he looked into herself, she wondered? She looked down to him with a new curiosity.

He had rolled upon his back, and, having plucked a small yellow flower from the lawn— in the dim evening she could only make out its color—he was touching it to his nostrils in order to perceive the delicate scent from the blossom; and this he enjoyed with his eyes closed and a smile of satisfaction on his lips. Plainly she was not within a thousand miles of his thoughts! A wretched sense of loneliness came upon Rose Kenworthy and in spite of the wide outlines of her father's house spreading against the sky, she felt abandoned and friendless in the world. The sight of the ranch-house roof reminded her for what purpose she had come into the garden this evening; and suddenly the thought of marrying young Glenhollen was utterly abhorrent.

"But the questions?" asked the man of the forest, snapping the yellow head from the flower and tossing it away. "This is the time to answer them all; I have promised you that."

She rested her elbows on her knees and brooded above him.

"Talking would never do. Talking could never teach me what I want to know; for it seems to me that you hardly know yourself—you're simply wandering along, keeping your eyes wide open to some things and closing them fast to the rest."

"Ah?" said he, and sat up. "To what do I close them?"

"To facts of all kinds—such as this: that you have to leave your fashion of life before long."

"Why?"

"Before you grow old, for one thing. When the animals grow stiff and can't kill, they live on roots for a while, and then they starve to death. Isn't that true?"

He shivered, and his eyes grew so large with melancholy that it seemed he had never thought of this before.

"You are putting the poison in the cup," he told her gloomily. "But women don't like to see men leave the beaten path. It's an alarming symptom when a man is able to live happily all by himself. Suppose that the fever were to spread!"

She wondered why she was not offended by that frank speech; but now as he sprang to his feet and leaned against the tree, she saw that she had truly stung him to the quick with her suggestion.

"I have kept my word and come back," he

150

said shortly, "but since you have no questions—adieu!"

"Wait!" she commanded.

He paused, fairly on tiptoe with eagerness to be off. To the girl, it seemed that if he left her now, half the happiness of life would be torn from her. What she expected from him she herself could not say; she knew she was fascinated, but could not say why. It was as though this stranger possessed a key to a mystery worth all treasure to be known.

"Instead of all the questions," she said at last, "I've decided on one thing: Let me see you work on a trail at night; let me inside your life from a midnight to a morning."

He frowned, and then he shook his head; but when she insisted, he pointed out to her gravely that it was a thing which could not be done far more for her own sake than for his. To let her hunt beside him for one night was nothing to him, but for her to come out from her home and remain away during so many secret hours might start an endless amount of gossip, if her absence were known. It was like trying to persuade the free wind not to blow; she brushed these petty objections away from her. No one would find out her absence, and if they did, she could tell that she had gone out for a walk on account of sleeplessness.

"There is some other reason that makes you want me to stay away," she told him frankly. "There is something that has to do with you.

But if you think that I cannot keep on the trail or that I'll spoil your hunting——"

He came back to her, at that, and sat on a mossy boulder, looking far past her to where the twilight was still living on the snows of the peaks, though the hollow was long since dead and dark.

"See what you are doing," he said gloomily. "I had made a free life for myself, doing harm to no one. If I give nothing to the world, at least I take nothing from it. Every day has begun with the midafternoon and ended with the morning, and if each day brought me a sound sleep, I was contented. I have learned to be happy on one meal a day—on eating once in forty-eight hours, even; and yet the winning of that food has been enough to make a reward for two days of hunting. See how complete I have been, not because I had a great deal, but because I wanted nothing except what a beggar would sneer at.

"Oh, I have known there are other things that other men live for and die for, but I have locked them all away; I have never been lonely because I have never allowed myself to have friends. I have shunned the very faces of men lest I should ever be hungry to see them. And there's no famine like the want of company, you know. It makes criminals come back to the place of the old home, where they know there is danger for them! And now," said the man of the wilderness, "you push open the door of my privacy and look in on me; but how can you tell that, having looked in on me once, I shall not suddenly stop in the middle of a trail and wish to see you again; that I may come back from a camp fire yonder——" and he pointed to the snowy crags above them, "and run down the slopes to find you, and find you gone?"

He stood up before her.

"If I see you again," he said, with the faintest of smiles, "I may be cursed with a desire to have you for a friend. That is why I never wish to put eyes on you again."

She considered him gravely, with just a touch of warmth in her face as she understood the singular nature of this compliment. Then she shook her head.

"You don't play fair," she assured him. "When you started to play the wild man, you guaranteed never to let the world in to peek at you; but now that I've found you it's only right that you pay the penalty."

She stood up in turn. "I'm going down to that hollow in the woods where I first found you. I'm leaving the house at midnight. Will you be waiting for me there?"

He did not return any answer more than a small gesture of surrender; and she turned from him and went back up the path toward the house.

Chapter Sixteen

The Whisperer's Trail

There is only one thing which can make two-handed poker exciting, and that is the presence of large stakes; but Jerry Monson and Montague were playing for matches. Not that they were short of money, but Monson, big, bland, and good-natured, had long ago discovered that his companion's irascible temper always grew white hot when he lost at cards, and therefore he steadfastly refused to play for money with Joe Montague. Perhaps it was owing to this diplomatic procedure more than anything else that they had remained friends for so long a time. For Joe, though his brimming spirits made him friends everywhere, lost them even faster than he made them, owing to his devilish temper.

So they shuffled and dealt and won and lost; but it made little difference how much the store of matches on one side of the board were diminished, since there were other boxes from which the heaps could be replenished. He who remained in possession of the greater number would, when the game was finished, be condemned to cut the wood and cook the breakfast for the following morning.

Even this small penalty was sufficiently heavy to make Montague lose all patience, and he began to show a heightened color as the game proceeded, and hand after hand turned against him. He was beginning to make sarcastic remarks about the success of his friend, so that Monson, who knew the other like a book, suddenly declared that had had enough of the stupid game and preferred to toss a coin for the onerous task of woodchopping on the next day.

The coin was tossed; and Monson, as he planned, lost. He pocketed that damage with a shrug of his broad shoulders and then, with a yawn, contemplated his blankets. In the long run, he would always win a more substantial stake from his impulsive and more generous friend; and what skill could not accomplish, persuasion would. Moreover, in case of need, the snaky skill of Montague in the wielding of weapons was a resource worth whole treasures.

Monson had hung up his gun belt; he had drawn off one boot and laid his hands on the other, and Montague was in a similar defenseless condition, when the door sagged suddenly wide and there appeared in the opening no other than Stew Morrison, with his great beak of a nose crimsoned from riding through the night wind, and his tiny eyes twinkling like the eyes of a bird. Moreover, in his immense hands, as reddened about the knuckles as his nose, he bore two big Colts, and directed one of each against the inhabitants of the shack.

They pushed their hands reluctantly above their heads, fighting against the temptation to make a sudden reach for their own guns or perhaps by a sudden motion overturn the stool upon which the smoky lantern was now resting. But they decided that to take a chance against such a known man as Morrison would be foolish in the extreme. So their hands went above their heads. Montague, more ready witted than his friend, gave the other the cue as to their line of talk.

"Look here, Morrison," he said, to the tall man, "ain't you been playing in luck, lately? Getting low in funds and have to turn in for this trade?"

Morrison bade them keep their hands above their heads and face the wall, standing side by side, and when they had obeyed he went over them carefully, took away their knives, and finding that they carried no other weapons, he allowed them to lower their hands and sit at ease.

"I got low enough," he told them then, answering the first question. "I turned in for a hard job, boys, but I didn't know that it would lead me to your way. You been raising a bit of hell, lately, ain't you?"

They carefully avoided looking into one another's faces.

"If there's any hell to be raised mucking in an old hole in the ground such as we got to call a gold mine," said Montague with a sigh, "you're welcome to the name, Morrison."

He looked behind.

Morrison nodded. "Been breaking ground hard, boys?"

"Pretty steady," they told him.

"I visited around at the drift and lighted a match, a few minutes back, to see how things was getting on. Didn't seem to me like you'd been walking very deep into the innards of the old mountain, boys."

"Quartzite ain't sandstone," Monson told him.

"And your hands, Joe," continued Stew Morrison, "don't look like you'd been raising many blisters with a double jack, lately."

"What's up?" asked Montague abruptly. "What are you drifting toward with all this talk, Morrison?"

"I aim to guess that you gents know, well enough."

"I ain't a bit of use at puzzles."

"Well, it looks to me like you boys ain't been making a living out of the mine for the past year."

"It's sure soaked up a lot of labor and gave us mighty little back," admitted Monson.

"You all had bank accounts to live on, I s'pose," said Morrison with all soberness.

"Not a penny," put in Montague eagerly, lest his companion should make a slip. "But we had a run of luck at the cards. Eh?"

He turned to his friend, and the latter nodded, brightening as he saw a way out of the difficulty.

"Luck at cards is a new thing for you," Morrison said to the spokesman. "Well, boys, I'm mighty glad that I happened onto you here." He almost smiled upon them as he spoke.

"What d'you mean?" asked Monson, now tormented by anxiety and by the yawning mouth of the revolver which gaped toward him.

"You couldn't guess," Morrison told them dryly. "You'd be mighty surprised, for instance, if I was to tell you that I wanted to know what you boys had been doing on Mackerel Mountain, a little while ago."

When such a blow is dealt, it is more than mortal nerves can endure perfectly; Monson withstood the shock well enough, but Montague, high-strung as a hair trigger, allowed his eyes to shift for a fraction of a second to his gun upon the wall. Then, realizing that his glance might have betrayed him, he turned pale; and having turned pale he realized that this pallor was eloquent, and grew as flaming red in an instant. He set his jaw as he glared at his tormentor.

"What in the devil is old Mackerel to Monson——or to me, leastwise?" he demanded.

The man hunter juggled the guns softly in his hands, and his little birdlike eyes bored into them.

"They's a dead man on the mountain," he told them soberly.

Again the blow told, and he followed it quickly with a third.

"I've just jogged down here to ask you boys what you might know about The Whisperer, you see?"

Montague was paralyzed, but the slow-thinking Monson now sprang to his feet.

"In the name of Heaven, Morrison, what d'you mean?"

"In the name of the devil," remarked the tall man, "I mean just what I say."

"The Whisperer? How should I know anything about him?"

"Sit down, Jerry. They ain't any hurry to say it at once. I just want a couple of parcels of news. I think that you boys can tell me—" He paused.

"Nothing," said Montague. "There's nothing to say, if you want stuff on The Whisperer."

"Feelings are running pretty high, right now,"

went on the man hunter, apparently breaking off at a tangent from his former course of conversation. But he came back to it at once. "If the pair of you was to be stuck in jail and the news was to get around that you belonged to The Whisperer's gang, I dunno what the boys in town would be apt to do."

Silence fell on the cabin.

"But if I was to learn something worth hearing about The Whisperer that——"

He broke off again. The wave of silence returned.

"Jerry," said Montague suddenly, "I can't stand it! I got to talk. Besides, the chief is off on us. You know what I mean. He's laying for us. I say—throw in with Morrison. By the heavens, we got to!"

A tremor of eagerness passed through the body of Morrison; he subdued it at once.

"Besides," agreed Monson, "somebody else must have blowed already."

He looked inquiringly at Morrison, and the latter merely grinned. "I'm waiting, boys," he reminded them. "I can take you down with me, or else I can leave you here, free as birds, and nobody to know that I ever come near you. All I ask is a chance to leave you boys alone and then to turn loose on the right trail for The Whisperer. He's my meat!"

"Heaven help you, then," broke out Monson. "You're chasing a devil."

"That's what they all seem like till they're

caught. But they tame down pretty well, I'd say! All that I've seen, do!"

Then came the flood of talk. It may be said to their credit that they were as close tongued as other men; but that dread of The Whisperer which had been inspired in them by the killing of Sam Champion whipped them on. It was at that point that they began their narrative, Monson carrying the burden, and Montague rushing in with bits of detail here and there. They told how with Champion and Tirrit the four had worked in unison for many years, and how finally they had joined the gang of The Whisperer in one unit. The deaths of the other two now left them in dread that The Whisperer had a deadly grudge against the old band of four; it was to protect themselves from slaughter that they talked now.

What they confessed then was the number of men in the gang, their addresses, the parts they had taken in different crimes, so far as the pair either knew or guessed, though they confessed that their information upon all the work except what they had undertaken with their own hands was extremely limited, on account of the adroit fashion in which The Whisperer handled his followers.

They were promised immunity by Morrison, now aglow with enthusiasm, as he saw himself fairly started, with exclusive information, upon the most important trail that he had ever undertaken.

"But how did you tumble to us?" asked Montague, tortured with curiosity.

"This way," said Morrison. "I picked up some trails running over the shoulder of old Mount Mackerel. I followed along without thinking anything about it. I came to a shack; there was nothing queer. I looked around at the mountains. There'd been a little landslide in one of the crevices that had brought down some tons of rock, but otherwise, there was nothing changed from what it had used to be. I looked around a bit more just out of habit, and then I caught a trail made by a hoss wearing a bar shoe."

"By the heavens!" cried Monson.

"Yep, it was your hoss. But I didn't know that then. Mind you, that was an old trail and old sign that I was following. But I rode along, working up it, not because I had any hopes of finding anything worth while, but just because I had nothing else to do. I was working on The Whisperer case, but I didn't have any idea where to start in. I worked up this trail just for the fun of it. It took me two days, boys. Two hard days, but at the end of that time I came on the end of the trail. I'd been following that trail mighty steady for a long time, working out where the bar had hit the rocks here and there, and so I came along, straining my eyes out till they ache right now.

"But I came up to your diggings, finally. I went into your shed a minute ago, and there, dog-goned if I didn't find that hoss with the bar shoe on the near forefoot. So I came in here to talk to you."

"But," broke in Monson, "how'd you know that we'd hitched up with The Whisperer?"

"Boys," said the man hunter, grinning, "I didn't know anything. I just had a hope that I might stumble onto the right thing. There wasn't anything else for me to beat up; I took a long chance. The bluff worked. That's all there was to it."

There followed a few half-stilled oaths; then came a long silence.

Presently Morrison continued; "Now, partners, you've started the music, and you got to keep playing for the dance. What I want to know is: how can I locate The Whisperer?"

They eyed one another, sullen, half desperate. Finally Montague shrugged his shoulders in surrender.

"Go find Lew Borgen and hound him a while," he said. "That'll land The Whisperer for you."

"Borgen?"

"He's in Cross City."

"What'll make Borgen talk?"

"Nothing. He's more afraid of The Whisperer than he is of hanging. But he's the only one who meets the big boss. Keep close to him and sooner or later he'll bring you to The Whisperer without knowing what he's doing."

This advice the man hunter meditated upon for a considerable time. Finally he rose, waved to them, and abruptly walked out into the night. The moment he was gone, Montague glided to Monson and whispered in his ear: "We got to get Morrison, pal. In your stocking feet; there'll be less noise. Now, out the back door!"

They scooped up their guns and skulked out the rear door of the shack; but it was only to hear the rattle of gravel as a horse near the shed where they kept their own animals, started hastily into full gallop under the touch of the spurs. They ran forward as fast as they could, but by the time they reached the farther side of the shed, Morrison was far away in the night. He had known them, after all, and had lost no precious time, relying on their good faith.

"Shall we send warning to Borgen?" said Monson at last.

"No," replied Montague. "We've stepped into the mud, Jerry. We got to fight on Morrison's side, now, and the sooner The Whisperer is bumped off the better for us."

Chapter Seventeen

The Unwanted Escort

When Rose Kenworthy reached her room, that night, she was in a wild turmoil indeed. She had told her father that she must have another day to consider the proposal of young Glenhollen, and not only that, but she had maintained a resolute silence in the face of his eloquent thunders. He pictured for her the glory of the united estates. But though his speech would have convinced any audience of voting citizens, it could not shake his daughter.

When she sat in her room, at last, she wondered what had made her so steadfast. It was not that she saw more faults in Glenhollen; he remained to her eye the same clean-minded,

165

straight-thinking young fellow she had always known. But now she knew that a man could be something more, and it was the man of the forest who had taught her. She sat for a long time at her window, with her elbows on the sill and her eyes on the stars above the mountains, trying to call up not so much his face as the strange and new emotion which had filled her when he was close. It was a difficult feeling to analyze, but in part it was like the eery delight of a child in a new home surrounded with new toys.

Yet there was a melancholy sense of loss, too, as though in leaving her, he had carried away part of her very self with him in his wanderings. Her sadness was the loneliness of the solitary mountains among which he lived. If the thought of the wild and free life made her look up with a smile, the thought of a bleak death with no hand to tend him made her look down again with a sigh. For this would be his end—a broken leg from a fall, or the sweep of a snowslide as he ventured up some terrible steep—and he would perish unknown.

She sighed as the picture came up before her, and again that strong impulse to meet him once more and try the power of persuasion to bring him back to the ways of civilized men rose within her; for he admitted that she indeed had some influence upon him—an influence which he feared so much that he shrank from her. At this recollection, she smiled faintly to herself. The wind swooping across the garden blew a delicate commingling of perfumes to her, and the stars were blurred by tears that came suddenly into her eyes. She wondered dimly at their coming.

Of one thing at least she was convinced; she could not venture out into the night to meet him, as she had promised. What mad impulse could ever have induced her to suggest such a meeting? Thinking back to it, with a little shiver of wonder, she felt as though it had been a different person who sat there in the garden talking with the wild man. So, taking a firm hold upon herself, she closed the window— for the air was grown a little chilly—drew a chair beside the lamp, unfolded a book, and sat down to read until the impressions of that day should have grown dimmer than a dream.

She had read until her eyes grew heavy, and she only wondered how she could find the patience to undress before tumbling into bed, when the great old clock which stood on the first landing of the stairs began to strike, and she counted the peals slowly, one by one, yawning. They reached ten; she rose from her chair, thinking that this was about the hour, when the eleventh chime rang through the house, and she started with surprise, half waking from her drowsiness. Then came the twelfth! The night had slipped away so suddenly that it was midnight before she had known, and now it was too late to dress for the outdoors and meet the man of the forest, even if she wished it.

The instant she felt it was too late, it became absolutely essential for her to go. She kicked off her slippers and stepped into walking boots; she cast a heavy cloak over her shoulders, jammed a soft hat upon her hair, and gave one glance to the night beyond her window. There was no sleep in her now. She was trembling and joyously awake and alive. She left her room, stole down the hall, and down the stairs past the round white face of the great clock which had called her forth. It gave her a ghostly feeling of a face behind her as she went on to the hall and then to the front door. It was heavily barred and bolted, but dexterously she drew the bolts without making a sound, and now she stood under the wide arches of the heavens.

She threw up her arms to them with a sudden delight, for the wind brought the strong and pure smell of the evergreens about her and far away, blotting out the stars in the northern half of the heavens, rose the mountains. They looked far huger than by day, and nearer, also; just as waves seem greater by night.

The stars were fading in the east, as the false dawn of the moonrise approached. She noted that with pleasure. Then she swung away at a brisk pace, for she knew the art of walking, and was presently deep in the gloom of the forest. She did not have to wander on to the far-off clearing, for as she came to the verge of the first little snow stream which angled through the woods, something like a shade fell across her path, and she looked up to find the man of the forest on the other side. He came lightly across to her, picking his way upon the stones without even looking down to them, so it seemed; then he stood close to her, and his voice was deep with anger.

"I came to meet you," he said, "but not an escort with you. If you did not trust me, why did you come at all?"

"An escort?" she murmured, astonished.

He shrugged his shoulders. "A sneaking fool," he said contemptuously, "is following your trail. Perhaps your father sent him—to take care of you!"

He said it in such a way that she could not avoid feeling his suggestion that twenty such obstacles could not control him if he chose to work harm to her.

She told him on her honor that she was not followed to her knowledge, and at this he drew a deep breath of relief.

"Walk straight on, then," he said, "and I'll handle this fellow."

"Not——" she began.

"There'll be no harm to him—if his nerves are strong," said the man of the forest, and before she could speak again, he had disappeared, with his usual mysterious speed, among the trees.

For her part, she obeyed his orders, but listening with keen attention to sounds which might rise behind her. She heard nothing. The man

169

of the forest had slipped back as noiselessly as a snake through the grass, until, reaching a great tree whose roots thrust out above the surface of the ground, he cowered close to the trunk, dropping into a formless shape in which even close study could hardly have revealed the form of a man. There he waited while a hurrying figure came out of the gloom, stealing rapidly ahead, drawn gun in hand, ready to kill at the first alarm. He stepped within six inches of the squatted form, strode on, and then halted in midstep and whirled. But the man of the forest was now in the air. The famous Stephen Rankin, for it was he, saw a flying shadow. Hard knuckles struck his right wrist, so that the revolver slipped from his numbed finger tips and dropped to the ground. Then the weight of the flying assailant's body smote him, and he went down without a sound.

The back of his head struck a projecting knot of a root, and the light of consciousness left him. When he recovered, and the dim understanding began to dawn on him once more, he was firmly bound, though the bonds were not drawn cruelly tight. He lay softly among delicate ferns; he was not gagged; and his assailant was gone. He could cry out for help if he chose. But he did not choose. For he was new to forest ways. In short, he was more formidable in the city than in the open, and to Rankin the dark began to fill with green-glowing eyes of beasts of prey, stalking close to spring at him. No, he dared not cry out for fear of guiding still other enemies to him with his voice. So he lay still, thinking, wondering.

What was the dark figure which had stolen out from the house of the sheriff sharp on the stroke of midnight and had then turned and waylaid him as he traced it and trailed it? It had seemed to the detective like the outline of a woman hurrying through the night; and yet it was certainly the steel hand of a man that had struck him down. Full of these gloomy reflections, the detective waited for an inspiration to release him from his difficulty; perhaps it would not come until the light of day put an end to his nightmare.

In the meantime, the man of the forest went back to the girl with his long and gliding stride, like an Indian runner. Most like an Indian he seemed to her on this night, with his long hair flying above his shoulders.

"What have you done?" she asked him.

"Tied him up," said he calmly. "He'll rest quietly there. Do you know him? A stocky man with a thick neck and a broad, thick hand."

"That's Stephen Rankin. He's working on the trail of The Whisperer."

"The—Whisperer?" gasped out the other. Then she knew that he was laughing by the way his head went back, though, as usual, his laughter made no sound.

Chapter Eighteen

The Enchanted Spot

The moon went up through the eastern trees on top of the mountain, and then it floated on into the heart of the sky, surrounding itself with a delicate mist of light and turning the sky from the deepest midnight blue to a colder darkness with a hint of steel in it. The stars went out one by one; first the smaller host of twinklers in one great brush of the moonshine, and then the huge yellow planets were drowned, until at last the moon was left without a rival. She was nearing the full, only one side of her broad circle being a little blunted, and she cast a light of wonderful brilliance down on the mountains. For the air

172

was clear and thin and dry; there had been no rain for some time; and there was no trace of moisture for the sun to suck up during the day, saving in the snows themselves, and in the snow-fed streams which trickled down the mountainsides. The silver moon was hanging well up in the sky when the two came into a little meadow—a space as level as though made so by man with the greatest of care, while the trees came down around it and paused in even ranks, all planting their feet on the outskirts of the ellipse of the opening and then daring to step no farther.

It seemed to Rose Kenworthy an enchanted spot, and she paused, leaning one hand against the trunk of a tree and panting; for it had been a hard climb to come to this place. Her heart was thundering; her face was hot, and for the last half hour neither she nor her strange guide had spoken a word. She half suspected that she was the victim of a practical joke, and that having promised to show her a specimen of his night life and of his hunting in particular, he would simply walk her to the point of exhaustion, and then let her find the best of her way home. But the arrival at this charming spot awakened new expectations in her. She looked again to the man of the forest, waiting.

He had stepped into the knee-deep grasses of the meadow and turned his face to the moon. The strong labor of that climb which had almost worn her out, tough and long-hardened little mountaineer though she was, had been as nothing to him. He had gone smoothly along ahead of her, and the light and springing step with which he moved had been the more maddening to her in her own weakness. Now he was scarcely breathing from those exertions, and gave himself over to the profound enjoyment which he seemed to find in the place.

"From here?" she asked. "Where does the trail go from here?"

"This is the end," said he.

"But your hunting——"

"I do it here, to-night."

She laughed, brokenly with her heavy breathing. "You are joking now, I suppose."

"If you want to see a slaughter, that may come later. I told you that I'd show you one of the trails that I live by, and here I've led you up to it."

She mused on him, ready to smile, still, and hardly knowing what to make of him.

"What is it you hunt here?" she asked at last.

"All manner of things—enough to keep me busy for a month, at least. You only see part of them at night, but there is enough if you know where to look and what to find."

He leaned and plucked several flowers from among the tall and feathery grass. "Here is wild carrot and goldenrod," he said, and he passed the flowers to her.

She took them in a wondering hand, still half ready to find a jest in it all; but as she looked at the flowers it seemed as if they were as truly enchanted as all of this pleasant meadow around which the loftier peaks went up into the heavens. Their colors, misted over with moonlight, were unlike any colors her eye had ever dwelt on before.

He began to walk on before her. Now and then he paused and added to the collection in her hands.

"Blue gentian—and wild asters—and here— breathe of this!"

He gave her a soft tuft of greenery which she pressed to her face and inhaled the rich fragrance of clover blossoms that the bees love. She had followed to the center of the little space, and here he dropped on one knee beside a rivulet which wandered through the center of the meadow.

"Here is the spirit of the place," he told her gently. "It has no voice for you, at first. But if you kneel here for a moment and listen— hardly breathing—"

She obeyed him. She kneeled by the edge of the water and listened, half closing her eyes, and presently she could hear it—a most delicate lacework of sound, rustling through the grasses where they advanced a step into the stream, and the easy coiling of the current as it turned the corners or swerved lazily toward the bank on either side; and now and again, when a breeze shivered across the grasses of the meadow, there was the faint lapping of small waves upon the shore.

She stayed there for a long moment, until the rivulet grew as a dream grows into a vast and winding sheet of water—a mighty river, going slow and solemn, toward the verge of the sea. The grasses became as tall and as dark as ancient forest along the banks, and the trees were hills.

Then he rose, the dream snapped, she stood beside him once more.

"Night is the time," he told her, speaking as softly as though he feared to frighten something away from her. "But there is quite another beauty in the day. There are a thousand insects quavering here and there over the blossoms, and great butterflies with wings as bright as aspen leaves in autumn. There are birds, too, and everything with some manner of a voice; it is a great chorus to think of, but in fact it is all so small and blended that one thought or lifting of the eyes will drown it all.

"Besides that is a drowsy time; it is so brilliant and so stirring that one begins to yawn, but at night there is no life here except the things which are rooted in the soil, and that is the best of all. If you want more, you can call up the other things with a thought, and see the ghosts of them. The birds are shadows, with the songs you remember coming into your mind, and the butterflies are tilting over the tops of the grasses as pale as moths in the moonlight."

He turned abruptly upon her, frowning. "These are some of the reasons I come here," he told her.

She nodded. "I understand, or try to. I've kept the mountains in mind just as things to climb, or look at against the sky; I've never dreamed of making them intimates, as you've done."

He sighed with what might have been relief. "I hoped you'd see——" He did not go on to say what, but added with a sudden change of voice and an enthusiasm which charmed her: "There are other things to watch and to know here, of course. Do you know how this meadow was made?"

"Made?" she asked.

"Of course. There's a reason for everything in the mountains, every valley and hollow and head of a peak, just as much as there are reasons behind the wrinkles in a man's face. A glacier plowed a hollow out of the bedrock just here. When it melted away, the hollow became a lake with snow creeks running into it, rolling down pebbles and a little sand. That formed a margin of silt along the edges of the lake; grasses and sedges began to grow. More rock and silt were washed down. The trees sprang up around the lake, and finally the lake itself was filled to the brim with sediment; it became as level as you see it; the grasses rolled across it, and here you are with a natural lawn."

"Have you learned all this since you came to the mountains?" she asked him.

"A person can't learn such things in a moment; I began when I was a youngster. You see, I'm going to explain myself so thoroughly that when I'm done you'll know me from end to end; then you can close the book and put it away, and we'll bother each other no more. When I was a boy, I was a bit frail; it was a mile from our cottage to the village where the school was, but even that walk was too long for me. It used to seem an age from the first sight of the little white house and the blue shutters to the time when I stepped onto the brick walk and heard the gate creak behind me. The doctor took me out of school and told my mother to keep me in the open.

"I had two years of it, and it was heaven. The place I hunted was a creek which ran through the hollow, west of the house. It had a young forest along its banks. There were a hundred kinds of birds nesting in the branches; there were a hundred kinds of lizards and water dogs, to say nothing of fish. Well, I learned that creek as well as I could. I was so interested that no weather could keep me indoors. Even in winter when the fogs blew in from the bay and rolled over the top of the hill and blotted out the walnut orchard, I still went out to the creek and found what I could find; and I was never disappointed. That was the time when I began to learn. So that when I was thrown into these mountains so many years later, I had starting points to go on from. Shall I tell you more about this meadow?"

"More about yourself. Much, much more!"

"That's too long a trail. This is the hunting I promised you."

"But I thought it would be——"

"A killing?"

"Yes."

"There can be that, too, if you wish. I expect to see an old enemy of mine here this very night."

"Without a weapon?"

"I have this," he said, drawing out a revolver. "Since the work is to be at close hand, it will do as well as a rifle."

He smiled down at her, though the shadows from the moonlight changed the smile into a sardonic mask.

Chapter Nineteen

A Killing

She was beginning to understand, now. This was no case of a lonely wanderer leading a sad life in a wilderness, for that wilderness spake as steadily and as clearly to him as did the printed page of a book to her. He could not be alone. Even a desert of sands and rocks was constantly telling him its story, speaking in a slow voice of hundreds of centuries; and here in the forest life must be passing about him in a joyous quickstep. No, it was she who felt a lonely and a barren life from the contrast.

She asked him when the hunting began.

"I am hunting now," he told her, "by waiting for him to come."

The Whispering Outlaw

"Does he move by the clock?"

"Very regularly, I assure you."

"Do you mean," she cried with a sudden horror," that it is a man?"

He shrugged his shoulders. "A man is not so very formidable," he told her. "There are other things in the mountains just about as terrible. For instance, if Madame Bruin should take a spite against me, I should be very worried indeed; a man would be much less. But mankind is the hundred-headed Hydra. If you strike off one head, two new ones spring out in its place. That is why I fear them. If you should let a whisper fall about me, it would be the end of me.

"For the sake of mere curiosity, men hunt through the polar ice to discover—what? The North Pole or the South? Oh, no! But simply to go where no one has ever gone before. They'd hunt me down. Ten fools might fail to find me; but that would only start a hundred trailing. They would keep at it day and night. When they found me, I could not escape. I'd be brought in for examination. They'd arrest me for vagrancy, I suppose!"

It was true enough, she knew. If she herself had merely heard of such a wanderer through the mountains, she could not have rested until she knew more about him. Indeed, here she was acting strangely enough to get at the heart of the wanderer, and yet the nearer she came to him, the more she found that was mysterious. After that he talked of other things. He pointed out the dimmer masses of the high peaks around them, which seemed to exercise a peculiar fascination over him. He told her how they were made—how the rocks had been folded up a mile higher than they now appeared to her; how the glacial age had sheeted the world with moving masses of snow, and snow compacted into ice, incredibly thick and terrible in power.

He told her how those glaciers had, at last, sculptured the peaks around them, and how the glacial age had passed; but still a few small ones at the very fountain heads of what had once been giants, continued to flow slowly forward, completing the more delicate chiseling of what the ancient glaciers had blocked out with great, rough strokes.

"But where will it all end?" she asked him.

"At sea level," he told her, smiling again. "Then another fold of rock will be pushed up in some other place, out of the bottom of the sea, perhaps, and the head of that mountain will begin to wear away just as this one has done."

It seemed that with the gesture of his hand, the mountains rose; with the gesture of his hand they sank again.

"The time is very close, now," he said suddenly. "My enemy is almost here."

So, with a quickening heart, she followed him behind a great rock.

"Lie flat," he told her, picking away some of the small boulders which encumbered the ground. "Lie flat; put your head in the hollow of your arm."

She obeyed him. Instantly he slipped to the ground beside her. Nothing was said for a time. She took careful heed of her surroundings. The rocks which gave them their immediate shelter must have tumbled down the side of the mountain; they were big enough to have crushed their way through the forest as though the trees were mere standing reeds, but they had rolled down here so long ago that the forest had sprung up again in the path of the flying ruin. They were on the very edge of the glacier meadow, with the trees standing tall and regular as raised lances behind them, and the moon, which shone against them, covered them with the shadows of the rocks like black paint. She could hardly make out the form of the hunter beside her.

"Watch the hilltop to the west," he told her. "But you'll have to change your mind if you expect to see anything."

"My mind?" she queried.

"Of course. Some thoughts are as loud as shouts. They tell people of danger that's coming; they tell animals even more, but even men catch some of the wireless messages."

"I don't understand."

"Haven't you ever watched a hound hunting a hare. It has no sense of scent to speak of, and do you think it relies on its eyes alone? Not at all! What makes it leave one field and run for the next? Only that some frightened rabbit in that field has sighted the hound and is crouching there with its heart beating madly. Its very fear betrays it, you understand."

"How horrible——"

"Everything that's true isn't pretty. Still more—why does a horse halt and refuse for a time to go over a shaky bridge, even though he has never been that way before? What tells him that the bridge is weak? Why does a dog run out from under a tree in a thunderstorm just before the lightning strikes that very tree? Come still closer home—consider how much we live by guess and by taking chance. It's as though we know that our instinct can guide us very safely and surely by avenues of knowledge which our conscious selves remain quite ignorant of.

"Have you never seen a gambler take his chance blindly? Sometimes he wins—sometimes when he is not concentrating too much on what he is trying to do! Why are the best gamblers the least excitable men? Because their carelessness enables that instinct to begin to work. I tell you, I have seen a man who now and then *knew* on what color the roulette wheel would stop! You will not believe at first, I suppose!"

"It bewilders me too much," she admitted. "I know that I've tried to rely on chance—never with any luck."

"Because you tried too hard. I knew a great gambler who was full of nerves. But he crushed away his nerves into nothingness by a tremendous effort of the will. He made his face immobile, and then he could win or lose with a smile or frown which had nothing to do with the true state of his emotions. No one could read his face. He kept his mind as empty as the brain of an infant, and he bet or did not bet according to what an instinct told him. When that instinct stopped speaking, he stopped playing. He played and won steadily for ten years.

"At forty he looked barely thirty. Then, in two years, he was smashed. His hair turned white; his face was filled with wrinkles, and the skin hung in pouches; and he died sitting in his chair after dinner, wrapped in a blanket for warmth, though it was a hot day. Of course it was simply the reaction of the nerves he had suppressed so long. The wave behind the boat became too great, overtook it, and swamped it.

"Now, if you look at the top of that western hill and make your mind a perfect blank, you will presently see something. But if you allow yourself to be consumed with curiosity, you may depend upon it that you will warn my enemy away!"

She obeyed him implicitly; for though she smiled at it at first, there was such an air of assured confidence about him that she could not help but do as he bade her. She made her mind a blank, thinking all thought away, making her very body limp.

"That is right!" she heard the faint murmur of her companion.

It struck her with sudden wonder; how, without turning his head, could he have known in what degree she had succeeded in obeying his instructions? Before she could resolve that question, a form appeared on the top of the western hill, just as the hunter had promised her, and paused there against the moonlit sky. It was no man, indeed, but a gigantic loafer wolf, with huge shoulders and sloping haunches—the head of a bear and the hind quarters of a jackal—a great, wise, cruel destroyer. He paused in this fashion for an instant.

Then he came down the hillside with his smooth trot, disappeared into the forest, and emerged with astonishing suddenness on the edge of the meadow. But now she could see him no more, for the rock blotted him from view. Neither could the hunter see, but suddenly he rose to his knees; there was a quick movement of feet through the grass of the meadow on the other side of the rock, and then the revolver barked, and the lone death cry of a wolf rang from mountain to mountain. Rose herself started up in time to see the monster leap high into the air. The wail and his life left him before he struck the earth, a limp weight.

"I saw him kill a yearling colt in a pasture one early summer dawn," he told her, "and I've trailed him since. A beast that kills a horse is a mortal enemy of mine. I've worked for two years to get him; and the wise old devil has known it all the time. I've found his trail at the edge of my camp fire in the morning, where he's stood and peered into my sleeping face, hungry to sink his teeth into my throat, but held back by something—Heaven knows what. Finally I stopped chasing him; I studied him.

"A man's mind is a lot more terrible than a gun to a beast. I learned his ways, the old fox. He killed on both sides of the range, you see, colts or calves, he hardly cared which. In crossing this part of the range I always found that his trail cut across this glacier meadow; perhaps he liked the taste of some of the grasses here. At any rate, there's one murderer less in the world!"

Chapter Twenty

Jeremy Saylor

He brought her back to the ranch house when
the moon, in turn, was beginning to grow wan
and fade to the dimness of a bit of silver cloud
in the sky. In the shadow of the house he said
goodby.

"I shouldn't have seen you again," he told
her. "I knew it after that very first meeting;
there was something fatal in you, and now I'm
afraid—I'm very much afraid that all the forest
and the mountains are dead things to me!"

She did not understand until she reached
her room and her bed; but then the truth stole
upon her with one delicious stride. All sufficient though he seemed, there was a flaw in the

armor of the man of the forest; he was beginning to fear her strength; and that was only a way of saying that he could not let her out of his thoughts—in one word, he was beginning to love her!

Rose Kenworthy sat up in her bed and clasped herself in her arms and laughed into the darkness as silently as the man of the forest himself. She did not even know his name; she could not tell how much of his story was a lie, or whether there was a grain of truth in it. That made her lie down again and draw the covers close about her, grown suddenly cold with the suggestion. She lay in the bed, turning quickly this way and that as she remembered bits of that strange night. She would never forget a word or a step which they had taken together. Then a shadow blotted her window. She looked up, and she saw that it was the man of the forest balanced there on the sill. But his face was pinched and haggard, and his eyes were deep behind a shadow.

Outside, the morning was brightening instantly. Suppose he should be seen? That thought drew her upright in the bed again, staring wildly at him.

"The moment I left you," he said gloomily, "I knew the truth. I've come back to tell you my name. I am Jeremy Saylor. I've come to tell you that Jeremy Saylor loves you. Why I should tell you, God knows! It isn't out of hope that you can care for a penniless vagabond of the mountains; but I've made a clean breast of it, and now, if you'll tell me plainly and bluntly that I've made myself ridiculous, perhaps it will give me strength enough to stay away from you."

He waited. But Rose could not speak. There was such a lightness of fear and of happiness in her mind that it seemed to her that the yellow sun of the midmorning was already pouring through the window—that a garden fragrance of roses was blowing through the room, and that the rattle of bird talk from the trees was the sweetest music playing over still waters.

"Or if you keep silent, Rose, I'll think that I may dare to take a great hope into my heart; and if I do that, I must have you or die for you."

Something stirred in the house; it struck a thrill of terror through her. "Go, go!" she cried to him. "They'll see you—they'll find you here and——"

"I don't care what ten thousand find or see. I only care what you——"

"Come back today——"

"Today?"

"Yes, yes—my father——"

"My God, Rose, does it mean——"

"I don't know what it means——"

"Before noon!" he called softly to her, and vanished from the window as though the dizzy height from the ground was no more to him than a mere step.

Yet it so frightened her that she slipped from the bed and ran to look. He was not on the ground beneath the window; but now she heard a faint, shrill whistle from the nearest of the encircling trees which swung around that side of the house, and there she saw him among the shadows, waving to her. She pressed both her hands against her lips and threw them out to him, and then, realizing what she had done, she sank into a chair and looked almost stupidly around her for help and comfort. She had a strange feeling that she was besieged with a hundred dangers, and yet that danger was a more delightful happiness than any she had ever dreamed of.

In the meantime, there was the interview with her father and the affair of young Glenhollen to be settled, and it made her shiver to think of the anger of the sheriff. So she dressed herself in the color she knew that he liked best, and sat down with him at the breakfast table in apparently the highest of spirits. That she was afraid of him was only one emotion, indeed; that Jeremy Saylor loved her, and that she loved him was the all-important thing.

Twice he tried to ask what she had decided about Alexander Glenhollen, and twice she avoided an answer, for she remembered her dead mother's wise saying, that a man should never be crossed until after his first smoke and his breakfast were completed. But when her father had finished his after-breakfast pipe and was walking in the garden, she came out to him and told him the truth. Her definite and calm refusal of Glenhollen left him staggered, and she sat down on a bench calmly, and watched, with a sort of scientific coolness, the rage gathering in his face.

The sheriff made a mighty effort and controlled himself so that he was even able to smile down on her and say in a choked voice: "I suppose that you've found a better suitor, Rose?"

"One whom I love," she answered.

"The devil!" thundered the irate rancher. He took a turn up and down the path, however, and so was enabled to control himself.

"Rose, I hear you say an impossible thing, but I'm trying to believe you. You say that you love another man?"

"I do."

"Where did you meet him?"

"In the forest yonder."

"In the forest! When?"

"On the night we rode to catch The Whisperer."

"Damnation, Rose, are you making a joke for me?"

"I am telling you the simple truth."

"Good—good! You met this—this—what's his name?"

"Jeremy Saylor."

"Ah? Who is he?"

"A young man."

"The devil! I mean, where does he live?"

"In the mountains."

"Confound it, Rose, don't provoke me too much. I'm bursting as it is! I mean, where is his home?"

"He has none."

"Eh?"

"He simply wanders through the forest."

"The devil; a penniless vagabond—a rascal who dared to——"

At this she stood up; for, measuring herself beside her father's rage, she was beginning to realize the full extent of her love for the man of the forest. She told her father calmly enough all that was in her mind—that she loved Jeremy Saylor; that she was of age to pick and choose among men as she pleased; that she loved her father and would gladly have pleased him with her choice of a husband, but that Jeremy Saylor was one step from wedded to her, and if need be, it would cost her no more than a sigh to leave her father's mansion and his fortune behind her.

"And follow this fortune hunter like a—like a squaw behind her man?"

"Like a squaw," she answered steadily, "if you choose to use that word!"

He might very well have fallen into a wild storm of abuse and driven her forever from his presence; but the effort at self-control had told so bitterly upon him that now these accumulated blows took his strength from him.

193

Besides, he was meant by nature to stand up against bluster, not against quiet firmness, and now he met in his daughter the same soft-voiced and iron strength which made him quail before his wife during her life. His strength suddenly left him, and he sank down upon a bench, pale and shaking. The bold dream of greatness which had been filling his mind since his first interview with young Glenhollen faded like a rainbow when a cloud blows over the sun.

Rose got on her knees before him, with tears in her eyes, holding both his hands and told him over and over that she would do anything in the world for him except to give up the man she loved. He asked her, still dazed, to tell him everthing, and she gave him the story word for word—all her meetings with this strange fellow of the forest, and every word he had spoken to her about himself.

Before she ended, he had fallen upon a new expedient. "Rose," he said, "God knows that at my time of life there is one thing dearer to me than all the rest, and this is to secure your happiness. But I've seen so many young girls throw away their lives and their happiness upon a chance love affair and a sudden passion, that I'm going to ask only one thing of you. When Saylor comes to the house today, I'll treat him with as much kindness as I can, but I want you to tell him that you cannot marry him at once. Let him live with us for a month, at least. At the end of that time, if you still find that you care for him, I'll never stand in your way. Will you do that?"

She gave him her promise with joy filling her throat and her eyes, and then the wily sheriff went to seek an ally. It was the detective, Stephen Rankin, who appeared that morning hollow-eyed as if from a vigil, and paler of face than usual. Also, he was strangely depressed and thoughtful, which the sheriff attributed to his lack of success, so far, in the chase of The Whisperer.

To Rankin he unburdened himself. To Rankin he repeated, word for word, the story which Rose had told him, and then he added: "What do you make of it? What is Saylor?"

"A cheat," said the detective without hesitation. He recalled his night in the forest with a shudder. "That any man could wander of choice through these mountains—it isn't possible, Mr. Kenworthy. He's simply lying to your daughter!"

The sheriff nodded and rubbed his hands together. "He's a fugitive; that's what he is, Rankin. I want you to find out what he's fled from. I want you to get on his trail, and if you can locate the place he came from—somewhere in the East, I suppose——"

"There ain't many walnut orchards in the East, Mr. Kenworthy."

"What have they to do with the place he came from?"

Max Brand

"You say he talked to your daughter about the fog coming in from the bay and rolling over the walnut grove on the top of the hill—that sounds like California to me, sir!"

"Eh? Perhaps it is! You have a head for these things!"

"Besides, there is only one place in California which they refer to as 'the bay,' and that's San Francisco Bay. I think I'll be hot on his trail in a week."

The rancher struck him confidently upon the shoulder. "Good! Good!" he said. "If you can fasten enough on him to break off this ridiculous affair by sending him to jail—you can name your own price, Rankin—by heaven, the ten thousand you want for The Whisperer is *nothing* to what I'm willing to pay. You're a made man, in short!"

Rankin rolled his eyes up to the blue of the sky and drew in a sharp breath. Already he was hungry to start.

"As soon as I've laid my eyes on this bird," he told the rancher with an oily malevolence, "I'll know something about him. Maybe—who knows? I might be able to recognize him! I've studied the rogue's gallery like a Bible!"

Chapter Twenty-one

Laughed At

He did not recognize Jeremy Saylor, however; the girl herself felt that she hardly knew him. It was her father who received the first shock. He came to the room of Rose with a singular light in his eye and told her that her friend had come. There was an odd emphasis in this, and she went down to Jeremy with an apprehension of—she knew not what!

She found Jeremy in one of the big parlor chairs, wearing the same tattered deerskin garments which he had worn before. How great and gaping were the edges of those rents, now! His black hair was combed out carefully, so that it fell to such a length that it brushed against his shoulders, and the light of the morning glimmered smoothly along its silky waves. But the long hair was not enough. In the deerskin jacket he had pierced a hole at a place corresponding to where the lapels would have been. Here there was fastened a whole spray of yellow flowers.

No wonder there had been the singular light in the eyes of her father. Her face became fiery when she thought that the cow-punchers had already seen that freak approach the house, and that they were soon to know that she was engaged to him. Then, beating down her self-consciousness as an unworthy emotion, she greeted Jeremy with all her heart in her throat.

But it was fearfully hard to talk to him. The free-swinging and courageous independence which had marked his bearing in the forest was quite dwindled, now, and he sat rather stiffly erect in his chair, looking about him as though he feared that the pictures hanging upon the walls might turn into enemies. The ceiling above his head appeared an impending danger. The place he chose for his chair was a secluded corner with the wall shielding him on either side.

She asked him what made him nervous, and he confessed that the presence of so many walls, so many corners behind which enemies could hide, was almost more than he could endure; he had been accustomed to too many years of the open forest or the desert itself. In the meantime, she suggested his stay in the house, according as her father had desired; a room was prepared for him, and he would be furnished with clothes and all things necessary to make him ready to appear among civilized men again; she would even guarantee him a barber.

But that suggestion he did not take at all kindly. Running his fingers through the black locks, he suggested that he would feel like a different man if they were shortened. A sudden little thrill of disgust kept Rose from pressing the point. As she sat there for an instant with her eyes upon the floor, she was on the verge of telling him that she had made a great mistake—that it must not continue for another instant, and that he must go back into the forest from which he had come. She hardly dared to glance at him again; but just then a bird sang at the window beside him, and when she looked at Jeremy she found him smiling, with his head thrown high, a fine and handsome fellow, surely!

There was nothing to do but to go through with it, she decided, though certainly the man who had won her love by night was far, far from this shrinking, unkempt fellow whom she saw by day! Jeremy was escorted up the stairs by a grinning servant toward his room. Then Stephen Rankin went past her, going down the hall, and there was a certain consideration in his eyes which made her certain that he knew. She paused; for he was about to go outside and tell what he had learned to the cow-punchers. Ah, what game they would make of poor Jeremy, and the yellow spray of flowers at his breast! She was on the verge of calling out to the detective and telling him to keep to himself what he knew, but then pride prevented her, and she forced her head high.

Then her father encountered her. He had the same amused look in the corner of his eye which she had seen in the face of Rankin. He took one of her hands and patted it, and then he began to laugh in the highest good humor.

"Honey," he said, "you saw this scared rabbit of a man by night and not by the day, and that's why you found something in him. It won't be a month; before a week's out, you'll be tired of everything except his flowers!"

He burst into a roar of laughter, which fairly shook the rafters above him. Oh, crowning humiliation! There was no answer which she could make. Only, she felt at that moment that if she had not despised Jeremy Saylor so much she might have come to hate him; he was not worthy even of hate!

Such was the feeling of Rose on the first day of Jeremy's coming; but she covered her feelings from the others; most of all she covered them from the observance of Jeremy. Yet strange, strange that he who was so keen eyed in the forest should be so dull in a house! At the table she passed through the most terrible ordeals. He seemed quite oblivious of every other person at the table; he even forgot his food. What she wanted to do was to shake him by the shoulder as a teacher shakes a refractory pupil, but instead, she had to sit patiently and endure those eyes which crushed all conversation at the table, and made everyone sit through long moments of anguish and shame on her account. She hardly dared to meet the eyes of Jeremy on such occasions, but when she did so, she discovered that they were not black after all, but that there was a shade of blue in the darkness.

"What was the business that you failed in, Jeremy?" she asked him one evening.

"I was a grocer," said Jeremy.

It was a crowning blow; somehow, it struck her to the very heart with shame. But other things were happening, in the meantime. The cow-punchers had received the news of the coming of the stranger who had won the heart of Rose Kenworthy with astonishment, with mirth, and then with horror. After all, this was not a thing for laughter. Upon it depended, in a measure, their own honor. For they felt that to allow a girl to throw herself away on such a fellow would shame them all, and forever.

"Shorty" was commissioned to examine the newcomer who had won the heart of the girl and then come back to report what he found out. When Shorty came into the bunk house he was as sick and pale and yellow as though he were ill indeed. He spat his tobacco into the stove and then addressed his silent and passionately interested companions.

"He ain't man," said Shorty, his upper lip lifting. "He's a rat. Darned if he ain't! He's got a soft, shifty eye. By the heavens, it's true that his hair is clean down to his shoulders and that he wears flowers in his buttonhole right along!"

The terrible news was digested in silence and with sick faces by the others. Then the foreman, Bill Matthews, arose and spoke from the bottom of his heart.

"Boys, he's like one of these here hypnotists I've seen that make fools out of people; he's hypnotized the girl. Looks like if we was fairsized men with fair-sized brains we'd ought to have sense enough among us to wake her up again!"

It was a noble proposal, and it was warmly greeted. It was decided that, in want of a good plan for the nonce, they would wait until occasion or inspiration served them.

A new rumor floated out to them the next day. It was said that the girl was already sick of her bargain, but that, having taken up the wanderer in the forest and brought him home, pride would force her to go through with a bargain of which she was already tired and heartily ashamed.

There was some basis for the talk. It had flowed out of a noisy interview between the rancher and his daughter. Jeremy Saylor had been there three days when the sheriff took his child apart.

"Rose," he said, "for Heaven's sake put an end to this foolish thing, won't you? We're all sick of Saylor; and so are you! Be brave enough to admit it and tell him to go back to the forests he started from!"

To this ardent appeal she made no reply; yet though she flushed, it was plain that she was a little thoughtful. Her father rashly went on, not content with the success which he had already gained.

"Between you and me, what Saylor is after is a little money. He knows that he can't marry you; but he wants to stay on until you and I are willing to buy him off, and I stand ready and willing at any time to give him whatever he asks. I'll even settle an income on him, so that he can live comfortably in any town in the land!"

But here Rose exploded with anger. For she was remembering the glacier meadow in the moonlight; and then the killing of the loafer wolf.

"I know that he's different from the rest of us," she told her father, "but a time will come when you'll see what sort of a man he is! When you find out, it'll be like the striking of a thunderbolt! I know what he is!"

The sheriff swallowed his retort, though he almost choked with the effort of it. He retired straightway to his room; but that day a rumor spread abroad and reached the bunk house in the form which already has been noted. Only the first part of the interview was reported. The latter half remained unknown. But had it been even whispered, it would have roused huge laughter from the rough men who listened.

But they were not finding a convenient time for a demonstration of what they wished to prove on the body of the man of the forest. For he kept himself well out of their hands. If he occasionally came near them, it was only to lean against the outside of a corral fence and watch, with wide, innocent eyes, while they roped a horse. Sometimes he walked for a short distance through the fields, but whenever he saw one of the cow-punchers coming toward him, he beat a hasty retreat.

"She's warned him of what's coming!" groaned Shorty one evening in the bunk house. "She already knows that he's a coward, and still she stays with him. There ain't nothing that can be done to open her eyes, boys!"

"You talk like a fool, Shorty," said the foreman. "When we've warmed up Saylor in a coat of tar, and feathered him down pretty well, I guess that she'll see he's black—I guess that she'll hear the rest of us laughing. No woman can stand having her man laughed at, boys!"

Chapter Twenty-two

Instructions

The work of Stew Morrison was made easier by the town in which he found himself. As a rule it was hard for him to drop into any community where he was not known to one or more of the inhabitants; and these quickly enough made him known to all the others in the place, so that his face and his accomplishments became household talk.

Moreover, it was known that he was busy on a criminal case, and this at once scattered every crook to the four winds to escape from his presence. But in the town where Lew Borgen lived, he found that he could be unhampered by such a misfortune. He was unknown as a blessed angel, and it allowed Stew to go about his work with a blissful sense of ease.

He simply found out where the grocery store and general merchandise establishment of Lew Borgen was situated, and then he rented a room in the house next door—a rear room which he told the landlady he preferred so that the eastern light might not waken him in the morning. In reality that rear room overlooked the living quarters of Borgen, who was installed in the rear of his store.

He was most comfortably fixed. There was a large backyard of half an acre in which there were two or three fruit trees, an arched way covered with grapevines, and a patch of green lawn. When Stew Morrison looked off to the burning sheen of the desert, reflecting heat waves as a mirror reflects light, and then down to the green of that lawn, it seemed to him that his very soul grew more cool and comfortable in that fiery western room of his.

Sometimes he saw the proprietor sitting out on the lawn under the walnut tree when the white-hot afternoon began to turn to a yellow light. Sometimes he would have his supper brought out to him there by a negro servant, whose only duty in the world was to attend to the wants of this one man. Now and again a gentle wind would blow to the window of Morrison the delicious fragrance of Borgen's cigar.

The Whispering Outlaw

He was the only man in town who could afford a personal servant and Havana cigars; and he indulged in both as though he had been born in the lap of luxury. Morrison, who knew better, grinned until those protruding teeth of his showed to the full. What they knew of Borgen in the town, he had learned, was simply that he was a fellow who had struck it rich in the mines some time before. Just where the mines were, no one seemed quite sure. Some said Montana; some said Alaska.

At least it was clear that the newcomer had plenty of money. Neither was he afraid to spend it. He had invested heavily in the ruined business of the storekeeper, but his prices were not only equitable, they were even a shade below the prices of other stores in neighboring towns. The townspeople were so surprised by this that some of them even expressed their wonder to him.

"Look here," said Lew Borgen, removing his cigar from between his teeth, "I ain't here for a minute to clean you out and move on. I'm here for life, you see? I ain't aiming to make a million in a minute. What I want is to make enough to live on. That suits me; and if it suits you, then we're all happy."

He was learning to smile, too, which was an art he had almost forgotten in his days of lesser prosperity. He was a bit fatter, too, and he showed the increase of flesh chiefly in his face. All of these things the detective noticed daily from his western window, looking down over the garden of the store-keeper. For his own part, he was like a hundred other men who had worked in the interests of law and order—that is to say, he had a thousand suspicions concerning Lew Borgen, but he was unable to prove a single one of the thousand.

He knew, to his own satisfaction, that the fellow was a crook, the more dangerous because he was so smooth and so consistently secret. But, even with the vital assistance of the suggestion of Monson and Montague, he felt that he had no easy task in apprehending The Whisperer, to say nothing of taking Borgen himself in the midst of a criminal act.

All he could do was to watch the man next door, and he spent every moment of his time in surveying Borgen. In order to do this, he simply gave out that he was suffering with lung trouble and that he had come West in order to enjoy the dry air. His cadaverous appearance amply reinforced this statement with every appearance of the most perfect truth. Stew Morrison was pitied and resolutely shunned, which was exactly what he wanted. He moved day and night whither he would, and no man asked him a question.

Yet, though he maintained his vigil for a full ten days, he found not a single scrap of evidence to reassure him that Montague and companion had told him the truth. Lew Borgen was playing the part of the retired and prosperous man of business, now amusing himself with the affairs of this little store. Finally, to get nearer to him, Stew Morrison ventured forth one day and disposed himself in the bushes under the fruit trees in the backyard of Borgen. He lay there, sweltering, all of an afternoon. In the evening he had the pleasure of seeing Borgen come forth and sit down near by, and whistle through his fat, thick lips, and smoke. But there was nothing except a few words at supper time between Borgen and his negro. Yet Morrison persisted, because he felt that he was now taking his last chance, and he wished to try it out thoroughly.

He came back the second afternoon and lay among the brush and was baked and burned by the heat, for the bushes only afforded him a meager tracery of shadow. But in the evening of this day Borgen did not come out at all. On the third day, to be sure, he came forth onto the lawn, but again nothing happened, the evening wore away, and the night came thick and black upon the place until he could make out only the outline of Borgen, sitting among the stars, and the red, round glowing of his cigar.

Borgen had twice yawned as bedtime approached; and then it was that Morrison heard the whisper. It came, to his horror, from the shrubbery not two feet away. He dared not turn his head, and yet it seemed to Morrison impossible that a creature could be there in the flesh and blood. No living substance could have forced its way among those brittle twigs and dead leaves without making sufficient noise to attract his attention. So, shaking with horror, he listened and watched.

Borgen had sprung up at the first sound, with a little grunt, such as men utter when they have received a severe shock.

"Good heavens!" Morrison heard the storekeeper mutter.

"Sit down, you fool!" said the whisper. It was a most faintly guarded murmur, rather than an entirely sibilant speech. It was far fainter, indeed, than a whisper.

Borgen sat down as though he had been jammed into the chair with an invisible hand.

"Someone may be watching," said the murmur. "You act like a jackass, Borgen!"

"It—it took me by surprise," said Borgen.

"Put your hand against your cheek, Borgen, when you talk; and not so loud. If you whisper loud enough for your own ear, you can lay to it that I'll make out what you say. Who's got that second-story room in that house?"

"A lunger."

"Sure?"

"Yep."

"He's got a nice view from that there window; he can see your fat back every evening, eh?"

Borgen shrugged his shoulders; but Morrison was prickling with horror. It was strange indeed that at a glance this fellow—and he could not doubt that it was the famous and terrible Whisperer himself—had pierced to the root of Borgen's danger! What was there about that window to seem suspicious? It was open, but every window was surely kept open in weather such as this! No, it seemed to be the result of instinctive caution and insight. Morrison felt that he was trailing a lion indeed!

"What is it?" asked Borgen.

"A job, Borgen, of course. Are you ready?"

"Of course! But——"

"Well?"

"Chief, I've got enough to quit on! I'm ready and willing to stop when you say the word. You can get one of the other boys to take the lead, but I have enough money to live on, and I'm losing my nerve!"

The Whisperer did not retort to this singular confession. He waited for a time as though digesting its full purport, and then he said: "Very well, Borgen; but once out of the gang, you never get back in, you understand? If you get out and then go broke, never expect to get back in to make some more coin. When you're through with me, I'm through with you, and forever!"

Borgen gasped out a faint protest. "If it's that way, chief, then I'm with you to the end."

"We'll both think that over. In the meantime, I've got a job for you."

"I'm ready, chief, for anything."

"You've got too fat and soft to do much but sit still," said the robber sternly. "But I want you to take word from me to two of the boys."

"Which ones?" asked Borgen, leaning forward in eagerness to propitiate this angered patron.

"Jerry and Montague."

"I can reach 'em by the morning."

"That's right. Make it a night ride and then back again. They mustn't know, in this here town, that you do a little wandering around by night!"

"Right, chief."

"Ride like the devil, then. Tell me first, are the two of 'em straight and square with us?"

"Yes. Straight as strings, both of 'em, so far as I know!"

"Darned strange, then, that they've both bought tickets East. Looks as though that meant running out on us, don't it?"

Borgen gasped with astonishment, and again that prickling of horror ran through the blood of the detective. He himself had just received word from the two that they were beginning to be afraid to stay in the country.

"Tickets East—the skunks!" breathed Borgen.

"And you thinking of pulling out, too; I see that I've been letting you all get too fat," said The Whisperer. "But go on and take this word to the two of 'em. Tell 'em that they're to start riding, tomorrow at noon, for Jessup. They're to go straight down the Richmond Road and through the Richmond Valley. Somewhere along the road they'll get their instructions about what they're to do and where they're to go. You understand?"

"Noon tomorrow—down the Richmond Road, through the valley, and instructions on the way. I understand, chief. Anything else?"

"Yes." There was a little and ominous pause, and then the bandit went on: "Tell the others what you know about those tickets East, and tell 'em that Montague and Monson are riding through the Richmond Valley tomorrow afternoon."

There was a slight rustling among the brush. "Chief!" breathed Borgen.

But there was no answer; The Whisperer had withdrawn as silently and as swiftly as he had come.

Chapter Twenty-three

At the Cottage

Rankin was a combination of bloodhound and bulldog; for, while he had a most true and delicate scent on a trail, he had the pugnacious qualities of a bulldog when he closed on the foe. When he boarded the train for California he was determined to stay with this work until he ran down the trail to the ground, if it required the rest of his life to complete the task. He had the sanguine expectation of the dropping water, which only needs infinite time to wear away the stone upon which it falls. Furthermore, he was exceedingly glad to be away from the mountain desert, for he felt that he was out of place there. In a city, he assured himself, he could never have been set upon, surprised, and rendered foolish, as he had been in that forest scene of unpleasant memory. But, once in a more civilized land, he promised himself that all would be changed.

When the train reached Oakland, he left it and traveled straight north to the town of Richmond; from that point he began his investigations. He hired a flivver and in the little car he began to work his way south over the network of roads. He had two things to guide him: The one was that the house he wanted was near a creek, and there are not so many of them among the sun-browned hills near San Francisco Bay; the other was the description of the house as lying near a village.

It made hard work for Rankin. Whenever he reached a town, he went out about a mile from it and began to trace a loose, weaving circle, going in and outside of the prescribed limits; for when Saylor had told the girl that he lived a mile from the town, he might have been merely approximating the distance; and his boyish recollection might have lengthened a half mile or shortened a mile and a half to the distance he mentioned to her. The detective took no chances. He dared not do so.

He was helped in his work by the people he met. Your true Californian talks to everybody and everything, it might be said. It is the last relic remaining in his character of the frontier disposition; for in the earlier days people were so few and far between that conversational moments were like rare gems, to be enjoyed to the utmost. Rankin found that the farmers stopped their buggies and hung a foot over the side while they chatted with him; and when he toured along bypaths, on foot, school-boys returning home in the mid-afternoon trailed along beside him and chattered like the birds in the trees above them. If he had kept a gossip book, he could have filled it at the end of every day with the odds and ends of information which he received.

Within a week, he found ten families named Saylor and all living near villages, but not one corresponded in all the details of a white cottage with blue blinds and a red-brick walk near a creek.

He pushed on, a little daunted, but still determined. He reached the Berkeley hills, beautiful beyond dreams, but beauty of scenery was not wanted by Rankin; he wished results and results only.

On the fourth day of that pilgrimage through the hills, he stumbled across the bottom of a dry slough, toiled his way up the farther slope, and then cursed freely at what lay just before him across the road. For there sat a little cottage painted white, with blue shutters, and behind the front gate the red-brick walk was embrowned by long weathering, and worn into hallows by many a year of use. It was just the place as Saylor had described his mother's house, but the detective had encountered half a dozen other places which equally well answered the description. All the setting was wrong.

What lay down the road he could not tell, and there might well enough be a village where it curved out of sight down a hill, but all the rest was wrong. Here was no creek by a dead slough which would run with water only during the rainy season; and the western hill, which must be covered with a walnut orchard, was as bare as the palm of his hand.

He turned back toward the cottage with a weary eye. It was a restful place. Upon either side of it arose an immense walnut tree, so very huge that the house shrank into a pigmy size in comparison. While the fields near by burned and quivered with the white of the sunshine, the intertwining branches of the walnuts drenched the cottage with shadow. There was a seat built around the trunk of either tree, and a modest little garden made a patterning of color in the shade.

All was neatly ordered and well preserved. None of the heads of the pickets of the fence which surrounded the place had been broken off—a great rarity indeed among such fences, he had observed—and the whole had recently been painted white so that it shone in the sun, doubly bright against the dark green of the hedge which grew immediately behind it. A schoolboy came past, swinging his lunch pail, and he stopped when the stranger hailed him, making great round eyes at Rankin and digging the rubbed toes of his shoes into the dust. He was as brown as an African campaigner; only around his eyes there was a faint rimming of white.

"Do you know who lives in that house, son?"

"Mrs. Richards," said the boy. "Ain't she home? She's always at home!"

His interest in such a strange possibility made him forget his shyness and with another question the detective drew him out.

"She's napping now," said the boy. "If she ain't sitting on the front porch sewing, or if she ain't pottering around in the garden, she's napping inside. Mostly she's around where you can see her from the road."

"You've been walking quite a ways," said Rankin, apparently changing the subject. "Far to school?"

"About a mile."

The heart of Rankin leaped.

"Is that in the town?"

"Sure. The school is right on the edge of town."

So Rankin, his blood quickened with hope, raised his eyes toward the top of the western hill and the barren level seemed to mock him.

"Tell me," he said desperately, "was there ever an orchard on that hill?"

"You mean the walnuts? They were pulled out last year. They never done no good up there. Pa said it was because the fog from the bay could get at 'em too easy!"

Rankin forgot the boy; he forgot the dryness of the slough behind him. For that matter, it might be referred to as a creek by one who did not care to be too exact. But here, beyond a shadow of a doubt, was his place; and coming upon it thus shocked him, as though it had been suddenly created here for his sole benefit. The boy went up the road, kicking through the dust, which followed him in lazy drifts, and now the screen door of the cottage, which opened on the front porch, jingled.

It was Mrs. Richards who stood in the shadow—a rather tall, stooped woman, with gloves upon her thin hands, a watering pot in one hand and a trowel in the other. Rankin advanced, and when he tipped his hat, she smiled down at him. It was such a kind and wistful old face that he felt rare impulse to wish to be of help to her. It was not hard to smile back at her.

"You're Mrs. Richards?" he said.

"Do you know me?" she asked. It was just the pleasant, quiet voice which he had expected. Such a woman, it was very possible, could, by too much mothering, produce that mild-eyed and shrinking fellow who called himself Saylor, and who had wormed his way into the affections of the rancher's daughter. Why had he changed his name then? Rankin was drinking deep of expectation every instant.

"I've heard about you in town," said he to answer her question. "I've heard about you as the lady who had the finest Virginia Creeper in the world!"

There it was, advertising its own existence well enough. The trunk was like the trunk of a tree, brown, and covered with rough bark. The arms stretched out with thick muscles on either side, and the smaller branches made a great network across the face of the porch, screening all within, and around the corners to an unknown distance, and up the roof to the very top. It was a magnificent vine, indeed, and now Mrs. Richards came down the steps and shaded her eyes while she peered up at it.

"It is a big one," she said, "but I've seen better ones, I think. Are you interested in gardens?"

"Very!" lied Rankin.

"Here is some pretty cosmos," she suggested with a sort of timid pride, and she invited him in by pointing to the clumps of it.

Rankin was instantly in the yard, and his clumsy hunt for adjectives to describe the delicate and feathery flowers and their dainty tints of lavender and pink and white might have told her he was only a pretender, but she was now in her own world, and too deep in her subject to be critical. She led him about the little place, while he exclaimed and smiled and praised and then waited for a chance to ask leading questions. It was too bad, he finally ventured, that she had no strong-armed husband or sturdy boys to help her turn the soil around that row of loganberries in the backyard, he ventured at last.

"My husband is dead, and my poor Charlie, but Jack is still alive—dear Jack!" she told him. "But he's in Canada, you know."

"Canada?" murmured the detective. His heart failed him.

"He traps there, you see, in British Columbia."

"A wild life, that!"

Jack seemed to like it, she told him, and, besides, though she often yearned to have him back, he had been so delicate of health in California that it was better for him to stay away. Upon this the detective pondered. Here was another bit of truth from the lips of Saylor to his fiancée.

"But Jack makes very good money," she told him. The conversation about the garden apparently had unlocked her heart. "He keeps the place up. Heaven knows what he retains for himself—he sends me so much, dear boy!"

Rankin seemed deeply touched by such an example of filial fidelity. He had an old mother himself, he told her, and it did his heart good to hear of such kindness from a son. Mrs. Richards was enchanted. Before another half hour had passed, he was sitting on her front porch sipping tea from a fragile china cup painted with flowers executed by the hands of the old lady herself in her youth! He tucked his heels under his chair and presented his best smile to her. He had himself been in the West recently. He had even been in Canada now and again. Then he had to answer many questions. Was the summer very hot? Was the winter bitterly cold? Were the people kind? Would a frail young man be mistreated by them?

He answered patiently. Most of his replies needed simply to be reassurances, and he lied liberally and with a loose hand when his information failed him. He made the winters in Canada fifteen degrees colder than mortal man ever endured; but he made up for this by telling her that such intense cold was nothing at all, "so long as a man dressed for it!" That was the solution. In short, he charmed Mrs. Richards with his omniscient touch. According to him, life even in the arctics was not very difficult. By this time, he vowed, her son was a stalwart from the life in the open.

"Do you think so?" she said, dwelling on his words plaintively. "But if you could see poor Jack, oh, he was always as delicate as a girl! He was a trial to raise! The picture of him——" She broke off.

"Have you a picture?"

"Oh, of course!"

"You've told me so much about him—may I see it?"

She was delighted to show it. She led the way into the parlor, where the half-drawn window shades admitted a soft light.

The Whispering Outlaw

"This is my Jack!" she said, and took the picture from the top of the upright piano, which was opened and dusted every morning and closed and dusted every night, but the keys of which were never touched from year to year.

The detective took the picture and examined it carefully. Beyond a doubt this was his man! This was Jeremy Saylor! There was the same thin face, the same pair of large, dark eyes. There was the same air of half-poetic, half-maidenly languor about the two. The likeness was unmistakable, though the wilderness had indeed darkened the skin of the wanderer and to a degree filled up the hollows in his cheeks.

Now something new caught his eye. It was of such importance that it made him run to the window and there examine the photograph in the sunshine.

"But," cried she, as much alarmed as though a bad symptom had been detected in her boy by the doctor himself, "what's wrong with Jack?"

"His hair," cried the detective, too excited to try finesse. "What color was his hair?"

Chapter Twenty-four

The Trap

The scruples of Stew Morrison were of a type easily pacified by reflection. His duty as a human being forced him to mount a fast horse and race with all speed to the assistance of Jerry and of Joe Montague. But his duty as a private detective to a client urged him to let Jerry and Joe take their fate as it might come to them. For they were the bait with which he hoped to catch The Whisperer himself.

Yet he conducted a silent debate with himself before he was finally and completely persuaded that it was indeed right to persist in his first inclination.

"How," said his conscience to Stew Morrison, "can you allow two men to ride to their execution, for there can be no doubt that The Whisperer means foul play!"

"If I can catch The Whisperer," said Stew Morrison to his conscience, "I'm doing a devil of a lot more for the world than if I save a couple of bums like them two, that are bound to come to a bad end sooner or later anyway!"

"You are arguing for the sake of the money you can make out of the rancher," said his conscience to Stew.

"I am arguing for the sake of everybody—for the sake of law 'n order," said Stew to his conscience. "This here I'm doing for the sake of mankind!"

That large idea finally convinced him that there was nothing right to be done except to go straight ahead and let the two miscreants pay, in the hope that in wreaking vengeance upon them their great chief might at last place himself within the danger of the law.

When the conscience of Stew was thus easily pacified, so that he could assure himself that it could never reproach him for whatever might happen to the pair who were acting as his associates in the cause of justice, he addressed himself with all possible vigor to the execution of the scheme.

His plan was, of course, to lie in wait somewhere on the sides of Richmond Valley, through which the two miscreants who had betrayed their leader had been expressly directed to ride. When Jerry and Joe appeared, he would wait until they were attacked by their terrible master and enemy, who was now prepared to avenge himself for the treason which he had so adroitly guessed at. The instant The Whisperer showed himself, he would be the target of the attack of Stew Morrison.

Though Stew was himself both a cool and a heady fighter, though he was a marksman par excellence, and though in a score of fights he had carried away no other damage than a few grazing wounds, yet he was not rash enough to consider himself a match for The Whisperer. He looked upon himself as a trailer in particular, and upon The Whisperer as a destroyer, in particular. Therefore he was determined to get aid before he struck at so formidable an antagonist, bearing in mind that there would be plenty of reward and of glory for him as the leader of the expedition. His followers would be to the world, numbers rather than names.

But it was necessary to find those who could be found ready and willing to act in such subordinate and yet dangerous capacities. Stew Morrison knew just where to find them. He spent the rest of that night and the next morning in routing out a group of vagabonds, men who had long lived by breaking the law, who had finally been caught, and who had purchased their safety by selling more notorious and more wanted criminals, their companions, into the arms of the law. In short, what Stew Morrison wanted were men who had played just such detestable parts as those of Joe Montague and Jerry Monson.

By a yet greater crime, because cowardly, such fellows saved their own lives but made themselves abhorrent to the whole world, both law-abiding and criminal. From the moment that it was discovered what they had done, it was impossible for them to mix with their fellows. Here and there, wretched and alone, they dragged out their existences, made savage and morose by the knowledge that all the world hated and dreaded them, and justly so!

Such men, knowing that they had nothing worth living for, were most willing to partake in dangerous adventures for the mere sake of money, and clever Stew Morrison had jotted down the names of all such in his mental notebooks. He kept them there ready to be used with caution, only now and again. But when a dangerous quarry was to be pulled down, he called upon these terrible and wolfish men, and they rode with him to the work.

He rounded up four stalwart graduates from the school of crime who had gone State's evidence and therefore lived in security until friends of the men they had betrayed should hunt them down and butcher them. They rejoiced in the names of Chris, Red, Lefty, and Porky. What other names belonged to them, they themselves had almost forgotten.

They looked very much alike. Their faces were lean, their hair long, their skins blackened with dirt and with sunburn, and their eyes too bright—too animally bright. Their horses were of a type, ugly of head, hunched of body, savage and treacherous of temper, but with the speed of deer and the endurance of wolves. With this body of light cavalry behind him, each man armed with a rifle and a revolver which alone of all the equipment was sure to be well cleaned and well oiled, Stew Morrison advanced toward Richmond Valley, and, before noon, they reached the post.

Richmond Valley was, in truth, no more than a cut between two great mountains. A glacier, perhaps, had pushed its plow of a million tons of ice through the defile, gouging out the valley narrow and deep—hundreds of feet deep. When the glacier melted, there remained a chasm of polished rock, smooth of side and of bottom. There the frosts of winter and the suns of summer began to work, cracking the faces of the rock until it was pried loose and fell away in boulders and great masses. By such means the walls ceased to be cliffs, in many places. The bottom of the defile was choked with fallen rock and boulders, among which the trail wound slowly back and forth. Speed seemed impossible through that pass.

The position which Morrison took up was about a hundred yards from the bottom of the western wall, at a point where a number of stone masses offered a perfect shelter for himself and his men, and, at the same time, enabled them to peer forth into every nook and corner of the pass. Also, from either side of the rock nest, it was possible to descend easily, down an almost smooth trail, to the bottom of the gorge. An ordinary horse, to be sure, would not be able to go down that descent without difficulty, but these hardy mustangs of Morrison and his followers were as sure-footed as goats.

Thus arranged, Morrison awaited the results with perfect confidence. The rifles of his men commanded the entire length of the pass. And what rifles they were! Not one of them but could bring down a hawk far above him, though shooting like lightning down the wind. Not one of them but would fire with as cool a deliberation at a human being as at a deer. To miss was not in their category of sins. It was highly improbable that The Whisperer would be able to do any harm to Joe and Jerry as the latter pair hurried down the gulch. The instant he appeared, he would be riddled with five rifle bullets.

In the meantime, he directed his men to keep a sharp lookout upon the upper walls and rocks of the ravine so that The Whisperer could not descend into it without being spied out. To be sure, it might be barely possible for a crafty man to work his way down the opposite side of the ravine to the bottom, shielding himself behind the rocks as he did so, unseen by the five pairs of eyes which were on the lookout. But it was highly improbable. For, coming there to lay an ambush, The Whisperer, and those with him, if there were any riding on this mission, would be apt to come boldly in and take his place. And before he took that place, he would fall dead.

Morrison described him exactly. "He's about middle height, but has very broad shoulders that make him look short. He'll probably be masked, with a black cloth. If his hair shows, it'll be red!"

There was no need to say more. Four pairs of eyes, each sharper than the eyes of an eagle, were now at work for him, and he could await the result. But the hot middle of the afternoon arrived, and still the great bandit had not been seen. Then the valley became an intolerable oven. But the shaggy creatures with Morrison sweltered in silence. They had the patience of beasts of prey; of a cat at the mouth of a gopher hole.

Then came a murmur. Morrison looked to the south and saw two horsemen slowly winding up the rise toward the mouth of the valley. Jerry and Joe had come at last into the trap. But where was the trap?

Chapter Twenty-five

The Last Killing

For there was, in fact, not a sign of another human being in Richmond Valley, neither had that battery of five pairs of hawkeyes been able to detect either possible trail or horse by which others might have entered the gorge. Lefty suddenly exclaimed: "By the heavens, The Whisperer got wind that we was coming, and he'll never show up!"

"He's got to show up," said Stew Morrison, shaking his head. "He's made the boys in his gang think that he can do anything, and that there ain't any fear in him. He's got to show up. He told 'em to ride this way, and he's got to meet 'em. He can't have 'em ride into his

231

camp some day and tell how he sent 'em out on a wild goose chase. He can't explain to 'em that there was five men waiting in the pass and that he didn't dare to show his face to 'em there. Because he's made 'em think that he's as strong as six hundred!"

This he muttered more to himself than to the others, as though he were simply increasing his own conviction without trying to greatly affect the minds of his comrades.

"This here Whisperer is a fake," said Porky. "Besides, he'd be a fool to try to play a lone hand with Jerry Monson and Montague. I know them two. They're hard, I'll tell a man. They're fast; they shoot straight, and they don't need no coaxing to get 'em into a fight. Nope, The Whisperer ain't going to tackle them two boys without some help at his back. Take it by and large, Jerry and Joe are better'n any two of us right here—not leaving out Stew, either! No man in the world would stand up to 'em——"

He had reached this point in his exclamations when there was a stifled shout from Lefty. They all stared down to the hollow and straightway saw a strange sight. There had appeared in the trail—not shooting from behind a rock, but calmly walking into full view—a short, wide-shouldered man, whose face was covered with a mask.

He bore no weapon in his hands, which rested upon his hips, but upon either hip there was belted a revolver, ready at his finger tips. He must have called out, for the two miscreants now whirled their horses about, and so they sat confronting their master.

"For Heaven's sake!" moaned Stew Morrison. "Get him now—salt him away—before he starts something with the boys!"

But the other four were already doing their best to get in a shot at the man in the pass. This was not so easy. For, instead of standing quietly, when they would have instantly marked him and dropped him with four perfect shots, The Whisperer was stepping lightly back and forth as he faced the two men on horseback just in front of him. He never appeared saving for just a glimpse as he turned, or as he passed between them. Had the group been a trifle nearer, even these glimpses would have been enough, but as all hunters know, snapshots are impossible at a considerable distance.

The result was that five rifles were handled with a burning impatience on the side of the gorge, and every second or so fingers would curl around triggers. But there was no shot fired. For at that distance the slightest error would mean a death for Joe or Jerry, whose backs were turned upon their secret and distant allies.

What was happening in the hollow of the pass it was not hard to guess. The Whisperer was talking as he shifted rapidly back and forth. The other two denied vehemently. They were being taxed home with something, and they were eagerly denying all guilt. Finally The Whisperer was seen to point, and the direction in which he pointed was toward that very group of rocks among which the five lay concealed. The two horsemen turned their heads in that direction. But apparently they saw nothing but the rocks, for all five were now lying low with the very greatest care.

Then The Whisperer for an instant stood still in his pacing back and forth and suddenly said something which caused the two to go for their guns. But The Whisperer was lightning on the draw; he fired twice, and the saddles of the horses before him became empty. In the same instant that his victims were plunging from their saddles, the bandit leaped sidewise among the rocks.

He escaped the salvo which now poured from the rocks above, as the five saw that they had no fear of injuring either of the men who rode in the hollow. But those rifles were aimed so quickly that every bullet missed him by inches only, and more than one of the marksmen above could have sworn that the outlaw wore armor which enabled him to escape such concentrated fire.

They now flung themselves upon their horses to rush to the bottom of the gorge and then press up the farther slope in pursuit. But they had hardly issued from their shelter when they returned to it pell-mell, for as the first rider darted forth, the air just in front of him was cut by a bullet. He recoiled and threw himself back upon his companions just in time to avoid a second shot which came even closer.

They now dismounted again, and hastily taking up position among the rocks which they had just prepared to abandon, they looked out upon the farther slope with malevolent eyes. Presently the fugitive was seen, a mere glimpse, as he turned the corner of a boulder. But three pairs of eyes caught sight of him at the same instant and three rifle bullets were instantly on the wing.

"I've got him!" cried Porky. "In the leg!"

"You lie!" shouted Chris. "I nailed him plumb through the head. Didn't you see him start to drop as he went around the rock?"

"It was me!" said Lefty. "I nailed him right in the middle of the back and after he dropped he didn't kick, you can lay on that!"

The three lunged out from cover. They were greeted by the light, swift hissing of bullets past them which splashed the hard brows of the rock about them with lead, and as they recoiled, cursing and gasping their surprise, the hurried, staccato barking of the gun from the farther side of the gorge came to their ears, repeated faintly up and down the gorge by echoes.

"Dead, is he?" mocked Stew Morrison.

"He's wearing a charm," vowed Porky, and straightway threw down his rifle and resolutely refused to fire another shot. "If I didn't nail him in the left leg right between the knee and the hip, I'm a fool and never fired a gun before!"

"But—" broke in Stew Morrison, and then interrupted himself by pressing the trigger of his rifle. "A clean miss again!" he muttered to himself. "No matter what you boys think, he's still living and moving, and he's halfway to the top of the gorge, now!"

"It ain't nacheral or right," said Lefty. "I never seen such a thing!"

But Stew Morrison had a cooler head, and he was not surprised at what had happened. He had more than once heard a party of hunters vow that each had planted his bullet in the body of a running grizzly which nevertheless refused to fall. Stew himself had trailed down the bear the next day, killed it with a slug through the brain, and found its body quite unscathed by all the bullets of the hunters, men who could ring the bull's-eye nine times in ten in shooting at a most distant target, so long as it were stationary and lifeless. But to shoot at a bear was different; to shoot at a man was another story, and to shoot at a hero, famed like The Whisperer, was indeed another story yet. So he smiled to himself and said nothing.

"That slippery devil is not more enchanted than any of us," he told his men calmly. "You're rattled, boys," and, he added diplomatically, "the same's I'm rattled. I've hunted on the trail a good deal before this, as maybe you know, but I never had anything unsettle my trigger finger like The Whisperer! That's how he killed Jerry

and Joe, just now. All he had to do was to up
and murder 'em—as easy as that!"

They were brought to their senses by this calm
talk of their chief's. Each man now set his teeth
and smoothed the wrinkles out of his brow and
the excitement out of his brain. Each now prepared to shoot as though at a mere target. But
the chances which were offered to them were
from this moment poorer and poorer, for as
the fugitive climbed higher on the slope, the
rocks sheltered him more effectually. He was
now level with his enemies, and they no longer
had the great advantage of delivering a plunging
fire against him.

"Work down to the bottom of the gorge!" cried
Stew Morrison suddenly, his brow puckering
with the realization that his man was about
to slip through his fingers. "Work down to
the bottom. Leave the horses here. Lefty and
Chris, you two start down on foot, and travel
fast. There ain't much danger of The Whisperer trying to shoot at you as you run. He's
too busy thinking how he's going to get over
the edge of that cliff without being seen and
dropped by us. The rest of you scatter back
up higher among the rocks. Get right on the
edge of the cliff. That'll give you a longer
shot, but a better target. I'll stay right here
and keep making noise enough for five if
I can."

He was as good as his word. He remained in
the original shelter, blazing away whenever he

had, or thought he had, a glimpse of The Whisperer. His two men above had hastily worked into position. They were barely on the edge of the cliff when they saw The Whisperer himself emerge from a nest of shrubbery and leap up against the face of the rock on the farther side of the gorge. There he caught a handhold upon a projecting bush and swung himself in a swift circle upward until his knee hooked over the jutting edge of a rock above him. From this precarious position he twisted himself up to the level of the top of the cliff and then rolled into safety upon the surface of the plateau.

In the meantime, of course, he had been the target for a steady discharge of guns from the two opposite, and from Stew Morrison. In all, nine or ten bullets were directed at him, but while his movements take long to describe, they were in reality executed with the greatest speed. Each movement was unexpected and therefore shook the trigger fingers of the marksmen. At any rate, The Whisperer rolled unharmed upon the surface of the plateau above, having accomplished a feat which made the whole country ring with his fame as it had never rung before.

It was to go far and wide, that tale of his adventure in the Richmond Valley, and how he had come into the valley in spite of the outlook of five grim men. How he had made his double killing and then gone back up through the rocks in safety. It was the sort of a tale which men, even big and strong men, told one another with frowning brows of bewilderment and cold in their hearts. It was not to be explained or understood. But that it had happened there was no doubt.

Most of the other deeds attributed to The Whisperer had been half mythical, half legendary. But it was known beyond a shadow of a doubt that he had robbed the sheriff's house in that wildly spectacular fashion, and it was also known that he had bearded the celebrated Morrison with four almost equally dangerous allies in Richmond Valley. After that, they were prepared to expect anything from the outlaw.

In the meantime, the two men who were sent into the bottom of the valley reached the bodies of Jerry and Joe first. Jerry had died instantly, and lay in a shapeless heap upon the rocks. But Joe had lived for a moment, and he had scrawled upon the rock with his own blood: "The Whisperer is——"

There, like Tirrit, death struck him down.

That, however, was not the only message left for the world upon this day. When Stew and his men climbed wearily up to the edge of the opposite cliff, not in the real hope of being able to find the trail of The Whisperer, but because they knew it was their duty to make some effort to follow the terrible bandit, they found a broad slab of granite almost like a prepared tombstone upon which the bandit had whimsically written: "Here lies the last of The

Whisperer, who will never ride again on the trail. He says good-by to his friends and his foes. They will never see him again."

"A joke," said Lefty.

But Stew Morrison took out his camera and made a careful photograph of the scratches upon the rock.

Chapter Twenty-six

Rankin's Discovery

"No matter what's happened to her," said Shorty, when he spoke in the council of punchers in the bunk house, "she'll be sick of him when she finds out that he's a coward! She won't be able to stand the sight of him after that!"

"How'll we show him up?" was the next question.

"Me," said Shorty. "I'll handle him. If one of the rest of you was to take a hand with him, him being so darned delicate and made almost like a girl, they might say that you was just bullies. But me, I ain't much bigger'n a minute, and if he won't stand up to me, she'll have to admit that he's yaller!" This suggestion

241

was greeted with the heartiest applause. Shorty looked like a grotesque carving of the body of a Hindu god rather than like an ordinary man. His body was like a doubled fist. His legs were bowed out beyond imagining. His face was of a monkeylike hideousness. Such was Shorty, who now prepared to step upon the center of the stage of this drama.

Rumor, which has a thousand tongues, and leaps from the beggar to the king, and from the king to the beggar in a manner and with a speed which men cannot understand—rumor brought a whisper to the rancher which he regarded as the best of good news. He sent for Shorty and spoke with him apart.

"Shorty," he said, "I hear that you are getting ready for a fight."

Shorty could not talk saving from the side of his mouth. "Wot you mean by that?" he said. "I dunno. I ain't hunting a fight, I'm hunting for a skunk."

The rancher was delighted. This passion of his daughter's had seemed to him a terrible, a disgraceful thing; also, it was a business calamity, and in both aspects it blackened the future of Percival Kenworthy.

"I've always," he said, "been very much interested in getting rid of pests of all kinds."

He looked upon Shorty and Shorty looked upon him.

"I guess, we look at this here about the same way," said Shorty, growing a little red.

"My boy," said the rancher, almost paternally, "it is plain that you understand—er—what is for the best interests of—ah—the ranch. I can only say—that is to say, I hope——"

He grew terribly confused. Finally Shorty extricated his employer by laughing.

"I guess," said he, "that if I was to take a day off for that skunk hunt, you wouldn't care none."

"Care? Shorty, you get a month's wages for that day's work, if you can show us the skunk!"

"There ain't no doubt of that," said Shorty, his far-away look fastened upon the gorgeous spree in which he would spend that kind donation of a month's wages for one delightful day's work. "I'll turn it up, the varmint, and you can all have a laugh at it!"

He turned away.

"Wait," said the rancher, with a palpitating heart. "When this is done, is it necessary that—that Rose should see it!"

"Sure," said the cow-puncher. "Ain't it her party?"

The problem remained with this statement of it. But Shorty lost no time. He haunted the ranch house awaiting his opportunity. It was really rather hard to find. The solitary Jeremy wandered off into the woods both night and day, sometimes with Rose Kenworthy and sometimes alone, and he was rarely to be seen lingering about the house.

Then a whisper came to the ear of Rose. She

went straight to her father.

"Dad," she said, "are the boys planning to make trouble with Jeremy?"

"Rose," he answered her calmly, and looking her full in the eye, "won't he have to take care of himself with the boys the rest of his life—if he's to own and run the ranch?"

That prospect seemed not to have occurred to her before. She remained on the verge of speech for some seconds, and then went thoughtfully away without having spoken another word. Furthermore, the rancher had reason to believe that Jeremy had not received any warning from his fiancée. It rejoiced Kenworthy's heart to see this first stirring of sense, as he called it, in his daughter.

Then came the dénouement. It happened with a terrible suddenness. The whole family was out strolling in front of the house and Jeremy was among them. Then, around the corner from the corrals appeared Shorty, mounted upon a buckskin mustang which was tying itself into artistic knots, impelled thereto by the left spur of Shorty, which was digging it cruelly in the flank. It brought laughter from the party to see the antics of Shorty in the saddle. He bounced dangerously high, but still he was not unseated.

Then, throwing himself out of the saddle, he let the buckskin race away with flying reins, while he waddled up to Jeremy Saylor with a face as black as night.

"Was you laughing at me?" he demanded.

"I?" murmured poor Jeremy. "Why, as a matter of fact——"

"You skunk!" snarled Shorty, and with his broad, open hand he struck Jeremy along the side of the face, a blow so heavy that the report of it was like a revolver exploding. And Jeremy reeled back a long stride.

Rose Kenworthy knew that the great test had come. The manliness of Jeremy in the forest she had seen with her own eyes. Indeed, there was something formidable and wild in him when the darkness had come over the mountains. But what would he do when confronted with the danger of another man? And such a man! Shorty's head came hardly to the shoulder of Jeremy; and Shorty as a fighter was ridiculous.

From her own part, every muscle in her lithe body grew hard. She saw in her mind's eye the flash of Jeremy's hand as he knocked the cow-puncher bleeding to the ground and then dragged him up again.

But this was not what happened. Jeremy Saylor merely stood in the distance, with his hand pressed against the cheek on which the blow had fallen, and his eyes fastened upon the ground. Shorty, swaying with his passion from side to side, was growling: "Only a yaller hound. Nothing but yaller! And laugh at me? Laugh at me? I'll take a quirt to you first!"

So speaking, he turned upon his heel, and

Rose, crimson with agony and shame, looked away, and saw, in front of the bunk house, the long semicircle of cow-punchers who had looked on and witnessed this whole drama of scorn. She almost fainted. But she managed to steady herself as she dragged herself away from the group and found a refuge in her room. But later in the evening she found Jeremy alone. A whole half hour had passed, but it seemed to her that she could still make out the faint outline of the horny hand of Shorty.

She wasted neither time nor words. She only tried to keep back her scorn.

"Jeremy," she said, "when Shorty struck you, why didn't you strike back?"

He looked at her with a sort of amazement. "He was much smaller than I," he said.

To hear that feeble excuse sickened her.

"Jeremy!" she cried.

"Besides, I was afraid, to speak to you plainly. Rose, I was afraid to touch him, for fear that I'd go too far and do him a serious injury!"

"Bah!" cried the girl, starting back from him. "You—you coward!"

She hardly saw him wince from the lash of those words, she had fallen into such a passion of disgust and sorrow and shame and rage.

"This is the end! I can never marry you. Good heavens, I'm almost grateful to little Shorty for having shown me the truth about you! I—I never wish to see you again—never! Never!"

She heard him crying out behind her. But she

hurried away from him. Then, in the silence of her own room, she cowered beside the window with her face in her hands.

"I'll never be able to face the world again!" sobbed Rose. "The detestable coward!"

But what miracles can be performed by determination of the spirit and nerves of iron? She forced herself down the stairs. She went into the dining room for supper. She was nearly stunned with astonishment to see that Jeremy Saylor was among those present! Then a swirl of horror passed through her mind. She told herself that the rascal had determined to stay on at the house even after his repulse. Perhaps he had it in mind to force some financial settlement out of her father's hand. She could not turn toward him; she could not meet his glance, and always she felt his appealing glance upon her.

"Like the eyes of a whipped dog," she told herself.

It was in the very midst of this confusion of mind, while she was taking her chair, and there was a bustle of everyone sitting down, that there appeared in the doorway the familiar figure of Stephen Rankin, the detective.

Behind him there were three others.

"By the heavens!" cried Kenworthy, already flushed with happiness as he saw that his house was freed from the incubus of a disgraceful marriage. "By the heavens, Rankin, I think that this is a great day in my life. I guess at good news before you open your lips!"

"Yes," exclaimed Rankin. "Good news, sir! Very good news!"

He rubbed his hands together. "I can tell you that The Whisperer will soon be of no trouble in the world!"

His three companions had sidled into the room and worked their way around the wall, unnoticed in the general excitement.

"You mean that the message the rascal wrote on the top of the cliff was true?"

"Without his knowledge," said Rankin, "it was true!"

He broke off and exclaimed: "Good work, lads!"

For here a rope had been dropped over the shoulders and the arms of Jeremy Saylor, binding those arms against his sides. He made one desperate struggle. Then he sat still with his eyes fixed steadily upon the face of Rose Kenworthy. She did not know how to interpret that glance. She only knew that it made her heart cold with fear and with expectation.

Rankin stepped behind the prisoner who had been thus secured. He deliberately fastened his hands in the long and flowing black hair of the man of the forest. With a wrench he tore the wig away and exposed a head covered with closely curled, red hair.

"Ladies and gentlemen," said Rankin, with all the calm which he could muster: "I present to you The Whisperer!"

Chapter Twenty-seven

Doubly Proud

How strange a difference the change in that one feature of his appearance made! Indeed, this very remarkably made wig had escaped detection from everyone, including Rose herself. The long and silken black hair had graced him with a sort of feeble effeminacy of character; but now these curling locks of red were like a waving fire upon his head. The slumberous black eyes, too, were now seen to be blue, and there was fire in them. All of this was the more shocking because, only the moment before, so to speak, they had been reviling and scorning this very man, this terrible and clusive destroyer, and they had been pointing the finger of

Max Brand

scorn at the man slayer because he had seemed in their eyes to be a coward!

There was little time or desire to ponder over this mistake and smile at one another, however. They were too much taken up by the aspect and the demeanor of this man. He remained bolt erect in his chair, never stirring after the first falling of the rope about his arms had made him helpless, and, all the while, his glare never left the face of the girl.

So grim and so fixed was that stare that the others, also, now turned with an eager curiosity to Rose Kenworthy. And they saw there enough to make them wonder. For she looked around her with the manner of one who has had a triumph. The very light of love was in her eyes; her cheeks were blooming with color; and the discovery that her lover was a bandit seemed to her of far less importance than the proof that he was a man!

She stood up at her place. "Dad," she said, "do you mean to say that you are going to allow a hand to be laid on your guest?"

"Be quiet, Rose!" said Kenworthy, doubly delighted in his character as a rancher and as a sheriff. "Be quiet, child. Do you suppose that this is not all of my contriving?"

He gave Rankin a glance which meant at least five thousand dollars to that worthy if he remained silent and allowed people to think that the whole work had been the plan of the sheriff. Rankin saw, and imperceptibly nodded, which was his method of telling the rancher that he knew and gave his sanction to the story, and at the same time he told the rest of the world that the cunning of the sheriff was indeed behind the capture. So the character of public benefactor was again bestowed upon Kenworthy, and he began to blossom in his part.

Only Rose Kenworthy seemed struck to the heart with indignation and shame by what she heard.

"Don't tell them such a shameful thing!" she cried. "Oh, dad, don't tell them that you kept a man under your roof as your guest and at the same time were preparing to arrest him!"

"Why not?" gasped out Kenworthy, and he flashed a glance around the circle of faces which reassured him. "Don't talk to me about fine points of honor. When I'm dealing with a man I treat him like a man, but when I'm dealing with a wolf, I treat him like a wolf! You, sir— Whisperer—Saylor—whatever your name may be, have you any claim to lodge against me for dishonorable treatment?"

This direct appeal seemed to make it possible for the glance of The Whisperer to leave the face of the woman he loved, and he turned his eyes slowly upon the rancher. From head to foot he surveyed Percival Kenworthy, and when he ended, he smiled, and looked back to the girl once more. Yet, had he opened all the thunders of sarcasm and wrath upon the head of the rancher, he could not have damped him as effectually as with this quiet and cold contempt. It made even the self-assurance of Kenworthy tremble. The color left his face. For an instant it became almost possible for him to doubt himself. But then the blood returned to his face.

"The rascal admits by his silence," he cried, "that there is nothing against me. He sneaked into my house under a false name. He lived here under a pretense—I only thank the dear God that he has been discovered before he worked any greater harm. Rose, what in heaven's name are you doing?"

She had run around the table and stood now behind the chair of The Whisperer, with both of her hands resting upon his shoulders.

"I've come to tell you," she said, "that I think it is a dastardly betrayal. But it shall never change me. If I was proud to let the world know that I was to marry Jeremy before, I tell you that I am doubly proud now that I know he is The Whisperer."

"Rose—go to your room—I forbid you——"

"I'll not budge! There'll be an explanation of what he's done that will satisfy me. As for satisfying the others, I don't care what they think!"

Here her father's fat hand fell upon her arm; she resisted only an instant, and then she went quietly out of the room. Only, at the opposite door, she turned back and exchanged a look with The Whisperer, while for an instant the sardonic coldness of his eye softened and changed to a wonderful tenderness. Then she was gone, and all attention swung back and centered upon The Whisperer again. Something seemed to be struggling in him for expression.

"Listen to me," said the sheriff. "Whatever you say may be used against you; you are now under arrest; but if you have a confession to make, it will be easier for your conscience. Whatever is said or done, for or against you, Whisperer, it won't keep you from hanging in due course. But in the meantime, speak out and make a clean breast of it. It will get you better treatment in the prison, and perhaps it may even get you an extension of time!"

This tender and insinuating speech, so filled with promises, brought a sneer of disgust upon the lips of the bandit. Again he regarded his captor with an expression of the most complete scorn. Yet he spoke.

It was odd that, when he spoke, though he used still the very gentle and quiet tones of Jeremy Saylor, yet his voice had for the others a different significance now. As the sheriff afterward expressed it, one could hear the purr of the tiger under the softness of the tones.

"I have one thing to say," said The Whisperer, "and that is to admit that I've done a bad thing. I've come into your house under a false name. I've lived here like a friend. I've— er—pretended to the hand of Rose knowing all the while that——Well, I can't go further into that. I'll only say this in my defense, that I thought that I was through with the life for which the governor will see me hanged; and I thought that it would be an honest man who would marry Rose Kenworthy. That's my only defense. Since I've told you this thing, I'll never open my lips to any living soul except Rose herself."

He uttered this statement with a perfect calm, neither threatening nor bragging, but conducting himself as though this were an event of no more than ordinary importance in his life. Having expressed himself in this fashion, he settled back in his chair, and from that moment refused to speak. They fixed the irons upon his hands, and next they searched his pockets and his person. They found to their inexpressible astonishment that the terrible outlaw carried not so much as a pocketknife upon his person, to say nothing of revolvers. He was quite unarmed. Neither was there anything upon him to suggest his identity. They went up to his room and searched it with the most minute care. But they found nothing in this place either.

When they came down to say this, there was the slightest lifting of The Whisperer's eyes, as though he was touched for a moment with surprise. But almost at once, he shrugged his shoulders again, and then was as silent as ever.

Nothing more was to be gained by question, but the little detective, Rankin, could not resist shouldering up to his prisoner and leaned above him.

"The gent you smeared in the forest," he said. "I'm the guy, Mr. Jeremy Saylor, Whisperer, Jack Richards."

Here the bandit started, and the private detective drew back with a malevolent grin to enjoy an expression of dismay. But it was gone as quickly as it came, and the face of The Whisperer was once more bland and calm.

"This'll be sweet news for your mother," said Rankin sourly. "She'll be all set up about the way her good boy works hard for her and catches so many furs every year that he'll be able to keep her so comfortably out there in California. But I'll have to let her know the facts. I promised her that I'd write to her if I should ever meet up with her son in the mountains!"

He laughed with the keenest enjoyment of this clever little jest.

He might as well have been addressing a face of stone, however, for The Whisperer continued to brood upon the infinite heart of space, and he heard not a word of the other, at least so it seemed.

So Rankin gave over, but not before he had muttered at the ear of The Whisperer: "There's the third degree waiting for you, cull. Maybe you're silent now, but we'll find a way to make you open your mug, you rat!"

Afterward, leaving The Whisperer under the guard of a dozen leveled guns, he had a conference with the rancher. The delight of Kenworthy, which had been kept within bounds while there were others around him, now broke forth in the most extravagant expressions of delight and satisfaction. He clapped Rankin upon the shoulder; he almost embraced the detective as he told the latter that the honor of his family, his dignity as sheriff, had all been saved by the ingenuity of Rankin.

He then demanded a narrative of what the detective had done and in what mysterious fashion he had been able to in the first place locate the identity of the bandit and even to find the home of Saylor at all. The answer of the detective was not too much in detail. He had come to find, in his professional life, that a mystery once explained away, can never be a mystery again, and that if the steps to the solution of a crime are given, every blockhead who hears the tale will think that he could have mounted the steps, or perhaps found an even shorter cut.

So the story which Rankin told was full of gaps. It seemed that by mysterious intuition he had floated west and west until he came to a place where instinct bade him hunt, and that there he had immediately found out what he wanted.

"But finally it all came down to the looks of his hair in that picture that I took down off the piano. It sure enough wasn't straight black hair. It was red, curly hair. The old lady told me what the color was. Right quick I jumped my mind back to The Whisperer. He wore curly, red hair;

he worked by night, mostly, just the way that Saylor lived. The minute I remembered that, I said to myself that I had everything smooth and easy before me. I turned around and I come back fast to the ranch, and on the way I pick up a couple of birds to help me snag the big boy— and you know the rest!"

"A marvelous story," commented the sheriff. "A very remarkable tale in every way. In the meantime, do not think that you are to suffer for what you have done. You asked in the first place a sum of ten thousand dollars. I know that some people would consider such a sum a fortune. But I, Rankin, do not. I hope that my ideas have expanded beyond such a point. What I wish to tell you now is that you are a made man.

"You shall never go hungry so long as you live. I give you ten thousand dollars this moment." Here he sat down and drew a long check book from his pocket. "But that is not all. That is only a beginning. I tell you freely, my friend, that if you had not come I might have had the misery to find my daughter married to the infernal rascal, and my hands thereby tied unless I wished to undo the knot by making her a widow—and that is too much to expect, even of a sheriff, eh?"

The detective allowed that it was. He heard the sweet music of the fountain pen as it crinkled across the surface of the check. He saw the check blotted; then it was extended toward

him, quivering with the emotion of the rancher.
Upon the narrow slip he saw the magic words—
written with thick strokes of ink—which made
ten thousand dollars be paid to Stephen Rankin
or the bearer of this check.

The detective folded the check and placed it
slowly in his pocket, and as he did so, while
he looked down to the floor, there appeared
between him and the carpet, a brilliant picture of a race course, of the noisy bookies,
of Stephen Rankin, resplendent in a brilliant
checkered suit of black and gray, strolling from
bookie to bookie with a fat cigar in his mouth
and fat rolls of money in his hand. He saw
his ten thousand bet; he heard the dull roar,
"They're off!" He saw his horse—it seemed to
wear blue and white—dance away into the lead,
float easily around the curve, and walk home by
itself. He heard the dull murmur of concern. He
found many haggard eyes fixed upon him. He
heard voices whisper great music as he passed:
"There goes Steve Rankin, the great plunger!"

Such was Rankin's dream.

Chapter Twenty-eight

A Hero

It was not for nothing that in business Kenworthy had always been a boomer and in pleasure a politician. He did not miss the chance of arranging a pageant around the capture of the notorious Whisperer. In the first place, he arranged to keep the great man in the ranch house until the next morning, and for that purpose he prepared a room in which four men, armed to the teeth, kept guard for two hours over their prisoner, after which their places were taken by four new guards, and so on through the night.

There was no lack of men for the duty of guarding, for the neighbors had heard the great news, and every man who rode into the ranch that night to make personal inquiry esteemed it a great honor to be allowed to sit guard during one watch over the famous man slayer and robber. It gave them a chance to ask him questions face to face, and though, to be sure, he always remained as oblivious of these remarks as though they had not been made at all, or as though he had been deaf, yet they could at least watch his face and his singular dark-blue, open eyes.

It was noted with interest that, cool as his nerves seemed to be, he did not sleep that night at all, but remained with his eyes open, staring before him. There was no expression in those eyes, however, neither grief nor fear, though many a one among the guards looked carefully to make out what he could. When they went out one of them tried to explain that absence of expression.

"The Whisperer," he said, "is an animal. That's why his expression doesn't tell you anything. Look at a dog's eye. Hard to tell whether a dog is going to bite you or lick your hand, if you judge by his eye only. It stays about the same. His tail does most of his talking for him, and his voice. Not like a man, where you keep listening to the words and reading in the eyes at the same time. That's the way with The Whisperer. He looks like a man, but he's got the soul of a beast. That's why he doesn't show anything that we can see. But down underneath you can lay to it that he's burning up, he's so scared about what's going to happen to him!"

This, however, was certainly not the usual opinion of those who watched over The Whisperer upon this memorable occasion. On the whole, they considered him to be a man in whose being fear did not exist. So they guarded him carefully during the night, talked to him or about him, and so saw the morning dawn at last over the mountains and turn them all pale and make the light in the room rather haggard.

Then the sheriff rose from a sound and a sweet sleep and prepared for the work of that day. It might be that Stephen Rankin had captured the prisoner of state, and it might be that the whole credit was due to Rankin, but the sheriff would not allow any other man to say so or even to think so. He let it be noised abroad that the whole having been done by his management, Rankin was hardly any better than a tool in his masterly hands.

In fact, such were the reports which he sent into town before his coming. Before that day was over, if Rankin had attempted with a sworn statement to prove his right to some honors in this matter, he could not have received them, so filled was the public imagination and the public eye by the figure which the sheriff made.

For Kenworthy arranged matters so that his cavalcade arrived in the town just at the lunch hour, when the appetites of men are keenest, and their minds are apt to be most awake, before falling into the lethargy of the hot afternoon. He now made his entrance in the following fashion.

First rode two old and experienced cowpunchers from the ranch, traveling at a considerable distance ahead of the main body. They were mounted upon ponies as shaggy and as wild of eye as those horses which the wild Tartars ride, and on which they once plundered half the world. Behind these scouts, who were armed to the teeth like the rest of the party, with rifles balanced across the pommels of the saddles and with revolvers stuck into their holsters or hanging from their saddles, came half a dozen of the neighbors of the sheriff, who were eternally grateful to Kenworthy from that day forward because he allowed them to appear before the public eye in this fashion.

Be sure that the face of each one of these riders was grim and set, as though he had just returned from the most terrible danger. Be sure that they looked upon the bystanders with haggard eyes, as though to behold those people for whose safety and well-being they had recently undergone vast perils and taken their lives into the palms of their hands. Behind these men came more of the sheriff's own cow-punchers, all tried and hardy men.

Surrounded by these, mounted upon a magnificent black horse which Kenworthy had furnished with a fine eye for the effect, appeared the terrible bandit, The Whisperer. Lest he should appear too young and inoffensive, the sheriff had carefully contrived that he should not be allowed to be shaved that morning, under the pretext that if he allowed the desperate man to have a razor in his hands, The Whisperer might cut his throat to avoid meeting his death at the hands of the ministers of the law.

It must be admitted that The Whisperer bore himself in a manner which made the sheriff almost love him, so perfectly did he fit into the picture of which he was, indeed, the central and most striking figure, save one. For The Whisperer, though his hands were secured in heavy irons and though his feet were bound together beneath the belly of his horse with a light fifth chain, was so adroit in his horsemanship that he controlled the magnificent animal upon which he rode entirely by the swaying of his body and the pressure of his knees. He rode the black, which was indeed a beautifully schooled animal, as though he had reins in his hands and a curb at the end of them to control the horse.

This was not all, for while his magnificent horsemanship enabled him to appear like a very part and portion of the animal which he bestrode, his upright and undaunted carriage, his thin and handsome face, and above all the expressionless eye with which he stared straight before him struck the people of the town dumb with horror and excitement. It was far more terrible than if The Whisperer had appeared before them as the wide-shouldered, massive creature which report made him out.

All of this was now shown to be merely a part of his dexterous disguise, for a little padding under the shoulders of his coat would furnish him with one detail of his usual appearance in the rôle of The Whisperer. By doffing his wig and allowing some of his natural hair to show, he effectually buried "Jeremy Saylor" behind him. Being so young he seemed more fiendish; and he seemed yet more unearthly because of the almost feminine delicacy of his features.

For, after all, who conceives of the devil as an old man? His wickedness is united to too restless a malice to be dressed in anything except the activity of a young body. So The Whisperer appeared to the townsfolk, like a very incarnation of the fiend. That was the way they regarded him.

Behind him came the rest of the sheriff's cow-punchers, for he had stripped his place in order to make the more formidable show. He had even forced his old blacksmith and his yet more ancient dairyman into service and had armed them to the teeth, like all the rest, though neither of them would have been able to hit the side of a mountain with a bullet.

Last of all, riding alone, mounted upon his finest horse, a gray thoroughbred, came the sheriff himself. He came last, as one might say, so that he might be removed from the public gaze. He came last, also, that he might act as the solemn and efficient rear guard which held off the assaults of the enemy. For, what gave point and reason to all this formidable equipment for the transport of the prisoner, was the rumor which Kenworthy carefully spread around that beyond question a terrible and immediate assault would be made by all the followers of The Whisperer to deliver their leader from the hands of the law.

There, then, came the rancher, with the cares of State manifest upon his grave countenance, now and then turning over his shoulder a wary eye, as though even now that they had entered the village, he half expected the dreadful foemen to rush in upon him—in which case his own experienced and fearless breast should receive the first brunt of the attack.

If there were murmurs of excitement and admiration and even of alarm from the spectators as the rest of the little procession defiled past them, when Percival Kenworthy appeared last of all, emotions were turned into a great enthusiasm, and the people could not refrain from opening their throats in a long and ringing cheer. More than this, the women shrilled at him and waved their handkerchiefs, or their aprons. They lifted their little children that they might behold the great and good man, the public benefactor.

"Oh, what a good man!" they cried to one another, after the noble Kenworthy had gone past them. "Oh, what a blessing it is that there are a *few* such men in the world!"

Percival Kenworthy, in the center of the little town, was stopped by a rush of admirers who pressed before him, heedless of the trampling of his high-spirited horse. There they compelled him to pause. There some of the best and leading citizens of the town pressed close to him and clasped his hand and told him that he was an honor to the whole range; that he was an honor to America!

He raised his hand in protest. He shook his noble gray head in protest at such devout compliments. He begged to assure them that he had done nothing beyond his duty.

At this, they thundered in his very face that he was no less than a hero. They then forced him to dismount. He was lifted again upon the shoulders of a banker on one side and an oil magnate upon the other. In this fashion he advanced down the street, and the yelling of the inhabitants made carnival in the air.

Stephen Rankin, smoking a cigar upon the sidewalk, watched all that passed with the greatest attention.

"By jiminy," said Stephen when all had gone by, "the old devil has squeezed pretty near ten thousand dollars' worth out of this here. He'll be a hero; he'll get his picture in the books."

Chapter Twenty-nine

Rose Visits Jail

Taken all in all, it was the greatest period in the life of Percival Kenworthy. He had always been surrounded by the admiration of others, but he was now surrounded by their worship. He had always imposed upon the women and the children, but now even the men followed in line.

The men of the cattle ranges and the mining districts had known and followed Kenworthy with interest for years in this fashion; when they read of him in the newspapers they nodded at the familiar name; sometimes his picture appeared. He knew the whole art of posing for newspaper pictures, with his face turned a little in profile, thrusting his jaw out to remedy its natural weakness, and gathering his brows in a frown, not of anger, but of resolute firmness. He looked, in that pose, exactly like a famous orator. Indeed, the sheriff looked so like a famous man in these clippings that he could not avoid keeping several of them with him at all times.

When he was alone in his office, or when taking a walk, he would take out half a dozen of the latest and favorite snapshots and thumb them over. In this way he was never without company; and he felt that the sight of his own face gave him an added strength; seeing himself at his best made him actually better; the man in the picture was so omniscient that the man in fact felt himself armed.

There was only one cloud upon his horizon at this time, which was the attitude of Rose. When he next saw his daughter he could not but expect that he would find her humbled and downcast, and that she would be forced to admit his provident care of her, which had torn the mask from her wooer. Instead, he found her merely silent and thoughtful. She had nothing to say, and she looked at her father as though she did not see him.

Then, the very next afternoon, she came to him and said that she wished to see the prisoner, the terrible Whisperer, in person, and alone. The sheriff asked her why, and she shrugged her shoulders. This made him consider, and he decided that, proud and self-composed as she was, she would not let him know what she thought, but that she wished to confront The Whisperer in person, and then denounce him face to face. Upon consideration of this, he allowed her to go, and sent note to the head jailer.

For there were many keepers of the little jail in the town, by this time. It was by no means the intention of these valiant people that The Whisperer, having been delivered into their hands, should escape. They surrounded him with something stronger than mere bars and bolts. They walled him in with the living might of armed men.

A little cordon waited constantly just outside the prison walls, lest he should dig his way through them; and in the jail itself, from which all lesser prisoners had been taken to another building, they kept a standing guard of half a dozen men who were constantly changed. They were not allowed to stand watch more than four hours at a time for fear that their vigilance should be dulled by sleepiness.

Rose Kenworthy arrived with the note from her father. "You may let Rose be alone with the prisoner for a few minutes," said the note. "To make sure, after she has left, you may search The Whisperer and see that she has left nothing with him by accident."

So Rose went into the jail and stood before her lover. He sat on his couch. His hands and his feet were secured by a vast weight of polished steel chains. He was calmly smoking a cigarette, lifting his hand clumsily every time he took a puff. But when he saw her, he sprang up, and the cigarette dropped to the floor.

She took hold upon the bars, and said not a word.

"Rose," said he, "whatever the others think of me, I have no care. But before I die, I want you to know that I fought against playing the villain with you. After the first time I saw you, I knew it would be dangerous to meet you again. I didn't wish to do it. But you know how it was. After the third meeting I was helpless. I loved you, Rose.

"From that moment I wasn't thinking of consequences. I wasn't thinking how you'd be damned if you should marry me."

"Is that all you have to say?" she asked, watching him curiously.

He sighed. "There's one more thing," he said. "I knew that the cow-punchers on your father's ranch were laying a plot against me. I knew that Shorty would try me out. I put away my guns for fear of being tempted to use them. I made up my mind that I'd try to be honorable by letting Shorty back me down before everyone. If that made you despise me, I vowed that I'd still stay on until you sent me away yourself and told me never to come back.

"That was just what was happening. You saw Shorty insult me, and you saw me swallow it.

Then you told me that you were through with me. It wasn't easy to do, but I stomached it. I determined to sit through that dinner, with everyone around the table despising me, and I should have done it, and in that way I should have undone all the harm I had worked in letting you care for me."

"Is that all you have to say?" she asked him.

He flinched and grew crimson under her blunt questions.

"One thing more," he said huskily. "A lot of what they've charged against me is true. But not the killings."

"None?" she said.

"Four," he answered. "My brother was murdered by four hounds. I killed them all. It was to handle them that I came West and arranged the whole thing. I killed the four, and haven't harmed another man. As for the robbing, I've given back to charity every cent that has come to my share. It was all a blind, Rose, a trap to catch the four, and after the four were caught—Montague and Jerry were the last of them—I was ready to stop. You know the message The Whisperer wrote on the rock?"

"Are you through?" she said.

He made a gesture of despair and surrender.

"Come closer to me, then," she said. "I don't want another soul to hear what I have to say."

He stepped nearer, the chain clinking.

"Nearer," she commanded.

He stood with his face against the bars, and suddenly her lips touched his.

"I came to tell you that, Jeremy. I love you. If they take you away from me, I shall never have any other man!"

"Rose! Rose!" he cried.

But she had turned away and hastened toward the door. Just before she reached it, she wavered so that she had to stretch out a hand and rest for an instant against the wall. Then she went on, and the door closed behind her.

She passed the men in the outer room, for this was the only way out of the jail unless the main door were opened. She made use of the tears in her eyes to smile at them, so that it would seem to them that her eyes were merely extraordinarily bright.

"She's through with that bird," said one of the cow-punchers who helped to stand guard that day. "She's sure through with The Whisperer. Doggoned if she didn't go out pretty near laughing."

"That's the way with a woman," said another. "There's only one good thing about it—they can't keep what they think out of their faces!"

They went in to The Whisperer to search him, however. But they could tell by his very attitude and manner that nothing had been done for him. All of his carelessness had left him. He sat upon the edge of his bunk with his face between his hands and his head bowed.

"She's hit him pretty hard!" said one of the punchers, who rejoiced in the appellation of "Slippy Pete." "She soaked him when he was down. Dog-gone a woman for not giving a damn about fair play!"

The others agreed with solemn nods.

"Whisperer," they told the prisoner, as they turned the key in the heavy wards of the lock which confined the famous criminal, "Whisperer, we got to search you. It won't take long."

The wretched prisoner did not seem to hear. They had to touch his shoulder, at which he looked up wildly to them, and seemed to search their faces without seeing them.

They raised him kindly to his feet, for there was not one among them who was not touched by the agony of The Whisperer. It mattered little that they could not understand his emotion as it really was. Then they searched him hastily, and, of course, they found nothing.

Then they returned to their outer guard room and conferred together.

"She put him on a fire and sure tortured him," they told one another gloomily. "Damn a girl like her!"

"But what was she to do?" asked Slippy Pete. "She couldn't go ahead and try to marry a gent that was going to be hanged, could she?"

Then he shuddered. "Damned if it didn't give me a chill to see a gent like The Whisperer plumb broke down," he murmured. "Think of him facing death and holding up the way he's been doing. Then along comes a girl and knocks him into a cocked hat! Seems like it's sort of unnacheral. Makes me kind of sick!"

"Look here," said the oldest fellow there, "you can't tell any man by what he does around a woman. Some of 'em are fools and some of 'em ain't. Sometimes the fools are wise around the girls, and sometimes the wise men are fools. Take The Whisperer, there. If you was to stick a gun under his nose and tell him that you was going to blow his head off, he'd laugh at you and tell you that he'd always hated the idea of hanging. But when this girl comes along and knocks the props out from under him, he ain't no ways fitted to buck up agin' it!"

They could not guess, one of them, that the agony of The Whisperer came from the sudden rebirth of longing for life after he had resigned himself for the end. He had said that his doom was written and sealed, and he had scorned to rebel against the inevitable, and here came a sweet vision of all that might have been, and made his heart shrink within him!

The word of what had happened was brought quickly to the sheriff, and he was told that his daughter had dealt The Whisperer a blow which had taken all the strength and apparently all of the courage out of the desperado.

He went with this tidings to Rankin.

"H-m-m!" said that clever worthy. "Girl sick, is he? Well, they all got their weak sides, these crooks. You go to him now, and you'll find he's soft. You go and sit down on his cot beside him and talk mighty brotherly. He'll tell you everything he knows. He'll confess all of his crimes. That's worth knowing. Afterward, I get my whirl at him. He gets the third degree from nobody but me!"

Chapter Thirty

Kenworthy's Mistake

The sheriff did not pause to think over this advice, for he considered the opinion of Rankin upon such matters as little short of inspirational. He straightway repaired to the jail and entered to extract from the suffering prisoner the final confession.

At the first glance, he saw that the wise Rankin had been right, as usual. For The Whisperer was a mere wreck of that proud self who had defied the world and death so gayly upon the day before. He was wilted upon his bunk. The weight of the irons seemed more than he could endure. His head was fallen against his breast.

The Whispering Outlaw

The sheriff put on the cheerful air of a doctor visiting at the bedside of a patient doomed by an inexorable disease to death. He banished from the cell room every other person. He unlocked the cell door. He entered and found himself alone, saving that the main door of the jail, through which he had rather pompously made his entrance, was standing a little ajar. He rather regretted that, but he did not wish to go clear back to close it. Outside there were half a dozen of the cow-punchers who stood on guard. One of them might be tempted to peek in and then would see the sheriff talking like a father to the poor prisoner, wheedling him out of his confession.

However, he sat him down as Rankin had advised, and began the conversation by laying his fat hand kindly upon the shoulder of the prisoner. That wretched man lifted his head and looked wildly about him. Then he made a feeble effort to rally, and even smiled at the sheriff.

"Friend," said the sheriff, "I've come to tell you that I'm very sorry for one thing: which is, that I had to allow you to be taken in my own house!"

The Whisperer waved his hand. The chain jingled.

"When I started the wheels of justice, they rolled on in their own way," said the pompous sheriff. "They happened to overtake you in a place which was not of my own choosing. In

277

Max Brand

the meantime, my boy, I've come to ask you what I can do for you?"

"Hang me this afternoon," said The Whisperer without an instant's hesitation. "Hang me this afternoon and get it over with. I'm—I'm going to pieces."

He closed his eyes and shuddered violently, and the sheriff himself turned pale. For he thought what an awful thing it would be if this reckless and daring man should indeed lose his nerve before the end, oppressed by the prison walls and borne down, perhaps, most of all by the last cruel words of Rose Kenworthy, and so die like a coward and lose the value of the last of his virtues—his courage!

Yet, thought the sheriff, turning the thought in his mind, it might not be a bad idea to let the imprisonment have its effect upon him, and disintegrate his obstinacy as much as might be, so that in the end he would confess everything, according to the degree of pressure which was put upon him with questions. Justice was not a thing of mercy, the sheriff told himself.

He said aloud: "That's blasphemy, my lad. When your turn comes—well, it comes. But who can be sure? For all you know, the governor may pardon you!"

At this The Whisperer actually recovered enough to smile.

"Why not?" continued the sheriff. "As a matter of fact, the men who are pardoned are usually the hard—I mean, the men who have committed a good many crimes. Just why that is, I don't know. Except that the governor often feels that what has been a strong force in crime may become a strong force for the good of society. Then, if you choose to confess everything, that confession would rake in so many men who would otherwise never be caught, that most likely the governor would think it worth his while to consider a pardon for you."

So spoke the sheriff, not at all what he thought. But it seemed to strike the prisoner most forcibly.

"Ah?" he said, and stiffened a little.

The sheriff felt that he had made a great impression. And indeed, so he had. He followed it up.

"Consider it from another angle," he said. "When a man is as well known as you are, Whisperer, people begin to think that there must be something to you—that there must be some reason for your crimes. If you had one murder—I have to talk plain English—against you, everyone would be for having you strung up. But since you have twenty—suppose we make it only that many—I think that everyone might consider you worth a new trial!"

The sheriff did not believe a word he had been speaking, at first, but he had talked on with such warmth that he had almost convinced himself. In the eyes of The Whisperer, he had planted a peculiarly thoughtful light. The prisoner began

279

to hold up his head and look around him. For the first time, he began to see.

He looked down, and the first thing he saw was the fat handle of a Colt looking up from the holster at the hip of the sheriff, for, since the capture of The Whisperer, the worthy rancher had taken more and more to the cow-puncher's costume.

With his ironed hands, the prisoner dipped the gun out of this scabbard. He did not seem in haste, and yet before the rancher could stir, the muzzle of the gun was nudged into the fat which covered his ribs.

"Now, you fat-faced fool," said The Whisperer soothingly, "stop thinking anything but what I tell you to think."

The brain of the rancher was more benumbed than his body could ever be. This was a thing which he would ponder over for many a day. He, Percival Kenworthy, had been called a fool!

"Take out the key for these irons," said the bandit.

The sheriff had thrust his hands above his shoulders to the full length of his arms. Now he started to draw down his right hand, but he hesitated.

"Go on," said the prisoner, with a broad smile. "I'll trust you not to make any funny moves—but just remember, Kenworthy, that I'm as good as dead now, and that if I've killed twenty men before this, I'd as soon as not make you the twenty-first!"

The Whispering Outlaw

This terrible confession of a crime-hardened nature made Kenworthy turn a pale green. At length his fear-stiffened fingers brought forth the bunch of keys. He was even allowed to use both hands to find the key, to insert it into the little lock, and to turn it. The manacles fell from the wrists of the fighter. How trebly terrible he became in that instant. In his left hand, carelessly, he now poised the weapon whose muzzle was digging into the aching ribs of Kenworthy. His terrible right hand was free, and it seemed to the rancher a separate agent of destruction, moved by an intelligence of his own.

"Now the leg irons," said The Whisperer.

The sheriff leaned and unfastened them. As he straightened again, upon his own fat wrists the horrible manacles from which he had just freed the arms of the prisoner were snapped. Then his no less plump ankles were secured in the same fashion. Last of all, his handkerchief was jerked from the breast pocket of his shirt. All of these things were done with such great rapidity that Kenworthy had really not sufficient agility of brain to keep pace with them.

That handkerchief was now wadded into a lump. Forefinger and thumb of iron gripped his lower jaw and wrenched it open. Into the gap the balled handkerchief was thrust, and next a second handkerchief was tied around his head. He was thus securely bound and gagged within the space of half a minute. Next the lean and amazingly strong arms of The Whisperer lifted the soft bulk of the sheriff and laid him upon the floor. Squinting sidewise, Kenworthy saw the light-stepping bandit make for the door.

Here he paused and looked back.

"If you yell out," he said, "or start kicking to make a noise, I'll turn and kill you before I start on the rest of 'em!"

Lifting the stolen revolver significantly, he scowled with murderous intent upon the poor sheriff. Then he was gone beyond the range of the sheriff's vision. He passed the door, behind which the six brave guards were waiting for the sheriff to finish his interview before they brought in the prisoner's lunch. He went on to the main door of the jail and looked out.

At the hitching post outside stood the beautiful black horse on which he had ridden into his captivity. Idling upon the steps, were no less than half a dozen more men, rolling cigarettes, laughing and talking to one another.

Worst of all, in case he wished to make a sudden break, the beautiful black horse was tied fast by the reins.

"We'd better go in and see how the sheriff is coming on," said someone from the guard room. "He seems to be pretty quiet by his talk!"

There were only half a dozen seconds left, perhaps. The Whisperer straightway used them. Upon his head he jammed the broad hat of the sheriff himself. Around his neck he jerked up the flaring bandanna which he wore. In this way the red of his hair was concealed. He now pulled the jail door wide open.

"All right, sheriff," he called, and waved back into the interior.

At this, every eye was turned upward. Not at The Whisperer, but into the yawning void of the big jail door where they expected the famous figure of the sheriff to appear at once. And, being so close, it might be said that The Whisperer was made invisible by the blinding light which surrounded him. He, being The Whisperer, it was impossible that he should be walking out of the jail door, calling to the sheriff. It was impossible, and therefore their eyes would not see what was happening.

He walked calmly down, making his steps draggingly slow. Very deliberately he unknotted the reins of the sheriff's horse. Very calmly he put his foot into the stirrup. Oh, murderous, slow seconds! How many deaths his agonized nerves made him die!

Then he knew by the sudden silence on the steps that they had finally centered all their attention upon him.

There came a whisper. He swung into the saddle.

"Hey, there!" called a strong voice. "Stop a minute!"

He turned deliberately upon them, at the same time jogging the black toward the corner of the building.

"So long, boys," he said genially. "I hope that I'll see you all soon!"

Just as he neared the corner, the blinding truth flashed upon every mind at once. There was a yell from half a dozen throats; half a dozen hands reached for guns. But at the sharp dig of the spurs the black had leaped past the corner of the jail, at the same time that the revolvers roared.

Chapter Thirty-one

Surmounting Obstacles

At the same time that this cry broke out from the men outside the jail, there was a similar frantic roar from within it. It was at exactly this moment that the guards, entering the main room of the cells to learn why the sheriff's talk with the prisoner was of such a silent nature, found, instead of two figures in The Whisperer's cell, no one at all. They plunged down the aisle between the cells, and there they beheld an awful sight. For they saw the fat body of the sheriff lying prostrate upon the floor.

Half a dozen hands readily lifted him up. But how could they immediately free him from his

Max Brand

irons? For the malicious criminal had carried the precious keys of the jail away with him, and with him, also, were the only keys within five hundred miles that could unlock those fetters.

But, in the meantime, while the guards realized what had happened, they raised a terrible whoop of fury. Their minds flashed far forward. They saw the entire town discredited forever on account of this jail break. They saw their pride dragged in the dust.

At this instant, even louder than their own, rang the yells of the startled cow-punchers outside the jail, and half a dozen Colts, barking as rapidly as agile fingers could press the triggers, poured currents of lead after the fugitive. Neither was the latter at once cut down, as could be inferred from the fact that the uproar at once turned the corner of the building and now wakened echoes up and down the entire length of the street. There began the hasty tattoo of horses getting underway, as riders flung themselves into saddles and began spurring, with one heel, before the other foot had reached its stirrup.

In the meantime, they had torn the gag from the mouth of the sheriff. He could only puff and gasp for a time, but then, regaining his breath, he roared: "Twenty thousand dollars for him, dead or alive!"

They did not wait to hear more. One and all, they turned and sprinted for the front door of

286

the jail, thinking only how much of a start the criminal and the lucky fellows outside the jail had upon them.

As for the sheriff, he had scoured the jail so effectually that there was not a soul to help him out. To increase his misery, the last man through the cell door had slammed it heavily behind him and left him doubly secured, both with bars and with fetters. The sheriff recalled that the miscreant outlaw had carried the keys away with him, and he considered the massive lock and wondered how long it would take to send to the nearest large town for a locksmith, and how long that locksmith would have to work before he could get the door open.

While all of this was going on, how many of the curious would assemble to stare through the bars at him? At this thought, the sheriff slumped down upon the cot with the cold perspiration running down his forehead. He felt that he was years and years older than he had been a brief five minutes before. He had lived longer in these briefly running seconds than in all his life before, multiplied many times. How completely was he shamed! He could remember only one thing, and that was the faint grin upon the face of Stephen Rankin as the latter stood upon the sidewalk and watched the triumph of the sheriff pass by him. Had Rankin guessed what was coming to pass so soon?

In the meantime, down the street whirled the cyclonic black horse with the rider flattened on his back, the reins gathered in one hand, a long Colt poised in the other, and the glitter of the sun upon the steel. Men said it was far less bright than the gleaming of his eyes, with the black mane of the horse sometimes blown across it.

Stephen Rankin had heard a noise in a distance. He had run out from his quiet little game of poker, and, by great good chance, he saw the fugitive speeding near, and he heard the thundered name from the crowd of mounted men who roared along in the rear of the black horse. He heard the name, too, shrilled by the tongues of women and children, sharper of ear than the men.

"The Whisperer!"

Rankin jerked out his gun. It was not a revolver. He had the highest contempt for such arms as a Colt. What he preferred was a burst of seven shots which followed one another in a thick stream at one pressure of the finger. He would probably kill both the man and the horse, but—why should such scruples make him hold his fire? He shrugged his thick, powerful shoulders. He remembered the evening in the forest, and the sudden, catlike speed of attack which had brought him down and made him foolishly helpless. So he picked up the automatic and drew a careful bead.

Then the muzzle of the Colt which The Whisperer carried jerked up, and vapor spurted from its mouth. A hammerlike blow struck Rankin on the right thigh, and caved in his leg. He went down with a roar of rage, and his automatic roared at the same time and pumped seven holes in the harmless surface of the earth.

Before so much as another thought could pass through his head, the gleaming body of the black horse had slipped away down the street past him. The Whisperer had passed another danger, but not his last. The whole town had been alarmed as by magic. The exploding guns; the beginning thunder of many racing horses; the yells of the chase, the shouts of commands— all of these had echoed far and wide along the single street of the village, and every man was up and roused and ready for action.

They turned, naturally, to the street. Had it been straight, the whole course of the action must have been clear to them, and The Whisperer would have been lost. But what they heard was a wild tumult of shouting and guns. Then a single figure upon a beautiful black horse appeared, riding at top speed. Whether he was the pursuer or the pursued was not quite plain. It was only certain that he rode like mad.

By the time each would-be aider of the law knew how to act and saw the streaming mob behind the fugitive, by the time, perhaps, he had recognized the celebrated features of the outlaw shooting past him, The Whisperer was gone and away, and the dust cloud was whipping up in his rear.

Such was the confusion of each man. But there was no confusion in the mind of Tony Caponi, the poor Italian who worked at his truck gardens in the early morning and half the night, so that he might have vegetables to peddle through the streets of the town during the day.

The instant he heard the noise he simply seized the bridle of his mule and wheeled the massive cart across the roadway. No matter what came, the ample dimensions and the Herculean woodwork of that cart guaranteed that it would give more damage than it received. So Tony Caponi stood to one side and folded his arms and waited. He was too weary to be excited. But he was at least mildly interested.

At once the flying black horse appeared. The rider straightened in the saddle when he saw the sudden obstacle before him. There was no way to get around it. For it was placed as though by the most dexterous design, just where the corner of the blacksmith shop jutted out on the one side, while the head of the mule reached to the front gate of Bill Sawyer's place. The road, in fact, was completely blockaded, and the black horse threw up its head, as though to inquire what was next to be done.

The outlaw looked over his shoulder. Behind him came three distinctly seen riders, slender, jockey-like figures perched upon blooded horses. For there was much good horseflesh upon this range. Many and many a cattleman had crossed thoroughbred stock upon the mustang breed, and produced a longer-legged, fast racer; and these in turn had been crossed again upon the thoroughbred until at last there was hot blood indeed in the veins of the progeny. It was not hard to tell that the fore-runners of the mob were so mounted. So was The Whisperer, himself, upon the black. But his mount was at least equaled by those behind him, and the weight of the three leading riders was less than his own. Speed of foot could never save him, then. Speed of brain must serve his steed.

He made his estimate quickly. Then he aimed the black at the lowest and narrowest point in the obstacle before him. In a word, he aimed at the mule. The black had never jumped in its life; at least, it had never jumped with a man on its back, but there was no hesitation in his heart. It gathered speed again as the spurs went home. It shook its valiant head, then gathered for the effort, and shot into the air.

For all its courage, that untrained power would not have succeeded had not the mule, seeing the flying danger approach, suddenly crouched. So he gave the black a few vitally needed inches. Even as it was, the heels of the good horse tapped on the backbone of the mule. Then the fugitive was over and struck the dust of the street beyond, floundered, regained balance, and darted away.

So the obstacle was surmounted, and now the worthy Italian was blocking the course of justice instead of helping it with a net to catch the prisoner. He saw his error at once, but before he could begin to swing the mule straight down the road, the dammed-up pursuit was boiling on the leeward side of his cart. Out of that press of horses, no one dared to attempt to jump.

One or two, giving up the effort to overtake the fugitive, and saying aloud that the devilish luck of the fellow would save his skin for this hundredth time as it had saved him before, rode to the head and back of the cart and pitched their rifle butts into the hollows of their shoulders as in the hope of taking a snapshot at the rider of the black. But the street curved in and out like a snake's track, and they took their aim only at the end of the black's tail, as horse and rider snapped out of view!

Now, however, the mule and the cart began to swing around. The instant there was room at head and foot, the cursing riders began to slip through, their spurs fastened in the quivering flanks of their steeds, and their resolution at the boiling point after this reverse at the hands of luck.

Instantly they straightened out on the street beyond. They rode like mad around the next curve, but alas, when they gained that commanding position, it was only to see that The Whisperer had indeed seized upon a most vital handicap. He was far ahead of them, riding the black smoothly and faultlessly, not needlessly

292

exciting the strong runner with whip or spur, but talking to him cheerfully, and so lifting him gayly over the miles.

Their hearts failed them; but, just when they were despairing, they saw that The Whisperer was not omniscient, and that he had ridden into a most fatal error. For he had turned into that lane which ran through the orchard of Bob Meany; and half the men among the pursuers knew well enough that this orchard had been flooded only the day before, that the lane was deep with mud, that the orchard ground itself was simply an impassable bog, and that they could choose their own footing on a safe lane to the left of the orchard.

Chapter Thirty-two

The Hidden Marksman

These wise ones veered to the left, accordingly, as they came opposite the mouth of the chosen lane, lay forward along the necks of their horses, and gave them both whip and spur to reinforce their spirits. Down the lane they fled, their horses grunting with the effort of every stride.

In the meantime, the rest of the posse shot ahead to the entrance of the orchard lane, unknowing of the muddy fate which awaited them there. But, around the first turn, they were in the midst of it. Of the first three horses, two skidded twice their own length, and then crashed to the ground and lay buried half the thickness of their bodies in the slush and the dobe. The others hastily reined in their mounts, and the hasty checking of speed proved even more fatal to balance and footing. In an instant the tangle of horses and men became terrific. It was here, in this famous pursuit of The Whisperer, of which all the range was to talk soon after, that Craig and Peters received broken legs each, and that a dozen others were put out of commission for active work by their injuries. This was a serious matter.

The remnant of the men who had taken this course picked themselves and their horses out of the muck as best they might, and pushed ahead without staying to succor the groaning men who lay around them. They gathered headway just in time to see The Whisperer's black shake the last of the mud from his feet on the farther side of the orchard, and come onto the dry land at a gallop.

But alas, poor Whisperer! How vitally the spirits of the black were spent by that struggle through the mud, and here upon the left came the better mounted half of the posse, as far behind as ever, to be sure, but upon mounts which had not had their powers vitiated by that struggle through the dobe, far worse than a climb up the steepest of hills.

He himself saw the mischief which had been done as soon as the gallant black straightened away. For the stride of the gelding was neither as long nor as springy as before. Then he heard

295

the roar of hoofs stamping up on his left, and, veering in the saddle, he thought they must be phantoms whom he saw coming so freshly, gaining at every stride. Then he understood; there had been another way through. There had been another and dry-footed way to come through the orchard, and the wiser half of the posse had taken that way!

From that moment he began to confess himself beaten. Not that he would surrender. Ah, no! He had resolved fully to die before surrender could be pressed upon him. He began to lighten his good horse. Behind the saddle there was a small pack strapped there for the sheriff. He cut it away. He went through the holsters.

There was an extra revolver in its heavy holster on the left side of the saddle as well as the one in his right hand. With a touch of his knife he cut that holster away. He slashed through the one on the right-hand side, for he carried that gun in his hand. He found the little hamper of cartridges for the sheriff's Colts. This he threw away without hesitation, for there remained five shots in the cylinder of his gun— four shots for defense and one shot to finish himself, he vowed. Then he went on through his own pockets. But there was nothing of weight there. Presently, however, he slipped out of his coat and threw that fluttering behind him.

Now, having lightened the burden of the black as much as he could, he took stock of the pursuit. They were coming hard and fast. The thick ranks were now thinned out. He would have been far happier to see a dense mob, crowding one another from the way, choking one another with the dust they raised, confusing each mind with their clamor and their disputes, wearing away nerves with their uproar and their excitement. But out of all the original mob, there remained only eight men.

These were chosen mettle, both man and beast; stupidity or faulty riding, or weaker horseflesh had been weeded out long before. They were all the more formidable by the smallness of their numbers, for there were not enough of them to hamper one another. Instead, each man looked upon his fellows, saw in them approved and distinguished men of action, and felt himself heartened for the work which lay ahead. That it would be stern work, and attended by some loss of life, not one of them doubted. Yet they hung resolutely to the trail, and danger would never throw them back.

These things The Whisperer judged perfectly, by swinging around in his saddle and surveying each rider in turn. He also saw that they were gaining steadily, not forcing their horses and burning them out in a sudden effort to run down the prey, but letting superior wind show itself over a course of time.

He began to jockey his own horse as well as he could, throwing his weight farther forward, so that it would fall more over the withers, and then swinging his body with the swing of the brave horse. But all would not serve, for behind him the pursuit still gained. They were riding as he was riding. Their horsemanship was fully as good, their horses were on a par with him, and in addition some of them were lighter weights and not one of them had put his mount through the mud of the orchard.

Considering these things, it was not strange that The Whisperer regarded himself as no better than lost, but he still fought his best. He turned into a narrow defile among the hills. Its upper head was the entrance to a sort of hole-in-the-wall country, full of trees and boulders, full of narrow passes and blank cañons. He knew all of that district as a student knows his book. If he could reach the head of that little valley he had a chance—say one chance in ten, of winning.

Having entered upon this final course, like the fox heading for its earth, he gave both whip and spurs to the black, and flattened himself to reduce the wind pressure against his body. The resulting increase in speed was sickeningly small. He had been riding far closer to the top speed of the horse than he had imagined. When he turned his head over his shoulder to look back, he saw that the others, indeed, were able to do what he could not succeed in performing. They were crushing out from their horses a spurt of racing speed, and they were closing in on him as swiftly and as surely as a hawk stoops to get at the bird which flutters beneath it.

He could not reach the head of the little valley. No, he could not even go half its distance! Then, to shut the last small door of his hope, a gun boomed up the valley, sounding from its very head, not the hoarse, sharp bark of a revolver, but the ringing report of a rifle, like two sledge hammers clanging face to face. He had not heard the bullet hiss past his head, however. Apparently the first shot had gone wide.

"It will be better luck next time," said The Whisperer to himself. "Better that it should end in this way. There's no other hope!"

So he sat up straight in his saddle, that he might present a fairer mark for the rifleman who lay among the rocks. But that marksman was wild indeed in his work! The bullet which The Whisperer would have welcomed to put an end to his career did not come near him. He groaned as the suspense increased.

But there arose, from the pursuit behind him, a sudden chorus of angry shouts. Then a volley of bullets whistled around him, not from the marksman up the valley, or any companions with him, but from the pursuit behind The Whisperer.

He turned his head and looked back, and he beheld a strange sight. A gray horse was running in the van, far in the van of the others. But its saddle was empty. And in the distance, well, well to the rear, was the late rider sitting upright on the ground, clasping his thigh with both hands. Beside him kneeled another—his bunkie, perhaps, or his brother, who let the chase go hang that he might attend to the injured man.

The eight were reduced, in this fashion, to six. Six men were more than enough to do the work which lay before them. But one of the six had dropped his reins and was clutching at one shoulder with the other hand, and the other five, with shortened speed, had brought out their own rifles from the cases beneath their knees and were opening a rapid fire upon The Whisperer.

Now, at last, he understood. That marksman who was firing from the head of the valley was not an enemy planted there by chance to cut off his flight. It was a friend, and the targets he had aimed his two long-distance shots at were the posse. How well he had succeeded with each shot The Whisperer had just seen for himself. And the rest of the posse, to avoid the deadly skill of this concealed enemy, had stopped trying to catch their man, and were content to risk their luck with a chance shot.

But chance is not very favorable to men who, having worked until their hands are shaking with excitement, their lungs panting, their eyes stinging with the speed of their riding, begin to shoot from the uncertain position of a saddle, on a dancing horse's back!

The Whispering Outlaw

Fine shots though they all were, their first volley went hopelessly astray. Then a third shot from the hidden rifleman at the head of the valley snapped the sombrero of one of them cleanly from his head. That was not to be borne, and, one and all, flinging themselves from their saddles, they dropped to the ground, lay prone there, and, resting their rifles upon rocks, they began to take cool and careful aim.

Small chance for The Whisperer now, with six deadly marksmen at work upon him! But he had placed some priceless yards between himself and the danger. Furthermore, he was now riding in a zig-zag course, swinging the black from side to side with as much agility as that weary beast could show.

One bullet sliced through his coat just under the pit of the arm. Two more sang at his ear. Then he saw that they had drawn their beads too closely upon him. He could not hope to escape from a second volley at such hands. He threw himself from the saddle just in time to have a slug nip his left ear at the rim.

But he was among the rocks, and he went forward at a rapid gait, running doubled over, to diminish the target in case the posse should see him as he fled, and dodging in and out and back and forth among the rocks and the boulders.

For a time the air fairly lived with bullets, singing about him. Then all firing ceased; they were waiting until they had an opening for a sure shot presented to them. That opening never came, for presently The Whisperer stood among the rocks at the head of the valley and saw, standing behind a great gray stone, no other than his old acquaintance, Lew Borgen, who had so effectually discharged his debt of his own life which he had once owed to The Whisperer.

It was Lew Borgen who was calling and waving to him, and, almost as welcome a sight as Borgen himself, there stood beside the big fellow two stalwart horses. It was as though The Whisperer had seen himself given wings to escape from the terrible danger which had been closing in upon him.

They said not a word to one another at that time. But they flung themselves into the saddle and rode like madmen until they had put ten rough miles behind them. Then they drew rein to breathe their horses and give them a swallow of water at a little rivulet.

Now Borgen stared wonderingly at his chief, whom he had followed vainly and blindly for so long.

"In the name of Heaven, Borgen," said The Whisperer, "what put you there to save my life and drive back the posse?"

"The mountains," said Borgen without hesitation. "I knowed that if you made a break it would be straight for the mountains. By the lay of the land I thought that a hoss would travel faster coming along up the valley than any other ways. Besides, I knowed that I couldn't be no good to you in the town. But outside, this way—— Say, chief, now that we're together and know that we can trust each other, we'll start the main clean-up, eh?"

The other shook his head. "The Whisperer is dead, Borgen," he told his lieutenant. "You'll never see his face again. Go back to your store. Live quiet. Go straight. You've got the makings in you of something a lot better than the greatest crook in the world—you can be an honest man, Borgen."

Chapter Thirty-three

Surrender

The governor, like most politicians, had been a lawyer in the beginning of his career. Unlike most politicians, he remained a lawyer to the very close of it. He lived not to win cases, but to advance the cause of Equity, that most difficult and unapproachable goddess.

He had become such a famous lawyer that a stricken and often-beaten political party, unable to face the next election with any prospects of success, had determined as a sort of drunken boast in the face of ruin, to nominate not one of its own men, whose stained and well-known consciences would keep them party tools even while they were governors, but to nominate a man who would have not the slightest chance of winning. Thus they could say that they had failed in the support of a good and a notoriously honest man.

So they nominated Peter Clark, simple as his name, little, withered of face and body, his whole physical existence dominated and over-balanced by the great brow which rose towering above his pale-gray eyes. He could not make a speech. He could only string together statements of facts; he had no opinions about mysterious things such as "government of the people by the people," et cetera, or about "the damnable trusts, who throttle our commercial life." For, in fact, he was used to prying into testimony, and he was not a man who surrendered easily to pressure, or who made up his mind easily or quickly.

This good and simple man had accepted the nomination not because he wanted it, but because his wife wanted it. He had never given way to his wife in his life because, dear simple soul, she had never made a request of him since their marriage. Therefore, this single wish he considered holy. He shook his head, shrugged his shoulders, and accepted, and allowed his thin, cold fingers to be gripped by the pudgy fists of the politicians.

They made no attempt to support his campaign and fight him into office. They knew that such an attempt would be foolish. Their man was beaten before he ran. But the opposition, the political party which had been triumphant for five straight elections, knew only one way to conduct an election. That was to smash at the enemy with obloquy and fierce abuse and slander, and to praise their own man. So they fell upon poor little silent Peter Clark. They abused him viciously through their hired papers. They sent a reporter to him who asked him insolently face to face what he knew about politics.

"Nothing, may God be praised!" said the good lawyer.

That statement elected him. The middle classes, who are ordinarily too busy making money to pay any heed to elections, were attracted by that phrase. Here was a man who knew nothing about politics. Here was a man of integrity as formidable as Gibraltar. Here was a man whose triumphs in the law extended through thirty years of victory. Suddenly the middle classes wakened. They formed themselves into voting clubs. They called to their aid that tremendously potent power of school children and school-teachers. They showed them the face of the swollen political boss who had already governed the State to its shame for two terms, contrasted with the lean features of Peter Clark, kept lean of body by intellectual strife.

The political swine rooted at the foundations of his strength in vain. They found his honesty was far stronger than steel. Their blasphemies did not need to be answered. Those who slandered him were ruined by their lies, and the governor was elected, though by a small majority.

For six months he did nothing. Then he ejected the entire corps of "bought-and-paid-for" officials, smashed to a thousand bits the elaborate political machines of the great corporations by exposing one or two weak links in their chains, and then declared that the ground was being cleared for work.

What work it was! All was done with the same care. He never moved until he had examined a case to the bottom. But when he had made up his mind, he went before the legislature as he had formerly gone before juries, and men were ashamed not to agree with one who so patently burned with the fires of justice and the mighty and holy love of goodness. They voted, one and all, for the measures. Step by step the State was purged. A thousand little grafts and iniquities were rooted out and done away with. Taxes began to pay for something other than their collections; roads, courts, public buildings began to be completed. Peter Clark became a political giant. He was one who existed without a party!

He lived in the most simple fashion in the world. He rose at the chill hour of six each morning. He worked at his studies—for he was still studying at the age of sixty!—until a half after eight, and then breakfasted more simply than a poverty-stricken laborer. After this, he read and wrote until noon. It was not until

307

noon that he was prepared to labor for the public. But, once started, he continued without abatement from that hour of noon until midnight—a long and mighty stretch of twelve hours. There was only one break in that period. Between eight and nine—for he partook of only two meals a day—he ate a repast as simple as his breakfast, and after it walked in his garden for a half hour.

There was only one thing he demanded during the entire day: he must not be disturbed during that walk after his dinner. For it was to the governor the one brief moment during all the day when his fancy escaped from his body, and his soul from the facts which surrounded it. Then, letting his thoughts fly away over the tops of the old trees, he sailed the Spanish Main of imagination.

It was more vitally necessary to the governor, in fact, than the brief six hours of sleep to which he limited himself each night.

It was during this very half hour that, upon this night of nights, he was broken in upon! Indeed, there were not six minutes of his time remaining when his old negro servant would come to the garden and call: "Sir, it is now nine o'clock." The dread of that voice was already falling upon the poor old man, when he turned a corner of the path down which he was walking and came upon the motionless figure of a man facing him. The governor halted. He had not the courage to speak, at first, so angry was he when he saw the shadowy form of the stranger, but eventually, when the passion left him at having his leisure broken—for he never uttered a word when he was out of temper—he said in his usual crisp and curt manner: "Well, sir?"

"How do you do," said the voice of a young man. "Are you Governor Clark?"

The governor grunted. Then he said as mildly as he could: "I am Clark. Who are you?"

"My name is Jack Richards."

"Mr. Richards, you have come to me in a time which I reserve out of all the day for my privacy."

"Sir," said the man in the dark, "I know it; and I have come because this is the only time in which I could see you."

"You are a very busy fellow, then?" observed the governor with an irrepressible touch of irony.

"I am," said the man in the dark.

"Doing what, Mr. Richards?"

"Avoiding your men, sir."

"Ah? What do you mean by that?"

"What I said, sir. Mr. Clark, I am generally called The Whisperer; and I suppose that name will explain to you why I have not come to you at another time."

"The Whisperer? The Whisperer?" the governor repeated growlingly. "Who the deuce— I mean, I have not heard of that name, Mr. Richards!"

There was a little silence.

"You have not heard of me—really?"

"No."

"But you have signed a blood warrant for me."

"Eh?"

"The State offers ten thousand dollars for me, dead or alive."

Here the governor clucked softly to himself.

"By the Eternal!" said he. Then he added: "You are the notorious outlaw!"

"I am."

"What do you expect to do here?"

"Make a bargain with you."

"Listen to me, Mr. Richards," said the governor, "I am a man who has never touched a weapon in his life, but if you think that I may be intimidated——"

"Sir," said the man in the darkness, "I give you my honor that I am not a fool. Only a fool would try to threaten you."

"Well, well! Come to the point, then. What does all this mean? What prevents me from stepping to that wall and pressing a certain bell which will surround that wall on the outside with secret-service men——"

"Your honor prevents it. You could not take an advantage."

"I see that you are unique. Come, sir. What is it?"

"A bargain, as I said before."

"To what effect?"

"To the effect that you grant me a pardon for my offenses."

"Ha?"

"I have said it."

"Sir, you are a notorious murderer."

"I have only killed four men."

"Only four? Only four? In the name of all that is sacred, Mr. Richards, do you confess that you have parted four human souls from their bodies and their blood?"

"I have had cause——"

"There are always causes. When a man denies my right to be governor, it irritates me; I may even wish him out of my way. I have had bad thoughts about a man who elbowed me on a street car. There are thousands of causes, but what cause can justify one for crushing in his hand that miracle of divine workmanship, a man?" His voice thrilled with emotion.

"Nothing."

"You admit it?" said the governor, stepping back a little, and seeming almost alarmed.

"I do, sir."

"Yet you say you have reasons?"

"When I was a fool, I thought I had reasons. I have repented."

"Ha?" said the governor again. "What made you repent?"

"A woman."

"The devil! I thought you were going to tell me a new story."

"No really good story has a new plot, sir."

311

"Mr. Richards, I fear your crime grows blacker. I might have some sympathy for an uneducated fellow, a man of wild brute passions, who knew no better. But you are a thinking man."

"You talk to me like a lawyer, sir, and not like a judge—or the governor I came to talk to."

The governor used a moment to swallow his anger. "It is true," he said a little huskily. "I have been talking rather like a child. Let me hear your reasons, then, like a judge."

"No, rather like the kind and wise man I know you to be. Here is my story. I was an invalid in a California village where I lived with my good mother and my wild young brother, Charles. He was as strong and as healthy as I was weak. He was my protector from the roughness of the world. That was why I loved him more than brothers are usually loved.

"He fell into wild ways. He was killed at last, in a gambling room in San Francisco, but he saved enough strength to live until he had seen me. Then he took one of my hands, and I saw him spending the last bit of his strength to tell me that four men, four Western cheats and rogues who dressed and acted the parts of cow-punchers, had enticed him into a crooked game, and then killed him when he discovered that the cards they used were marked. He described them; he gave me the nicknames they called one another. He begged me not to let him die without being avenged.

"I thought that the law would handle them. But when I had waited for a month and the law had no trace of the killers, I made my plan. I decided that I should make myself a man and a formidable man in the same sense that those expert gunmen and sneaks were formidable when they killed my brother. So I went to that part of the West where the criminals were who had killed Charles, and as I could not afford to have myself become known, I began to live by night, obscurely.

"I taught myself to live as the beasts live. I learned to hunt, trap. I became an expert marksman. Then I conceived the scheme of drawing in these four men—for by this time I had been able to guess at their identity—to a mysterious gang of which I could be the chief, while still remaining unseen and almost unknown.

"That was the origin of the gang you heard of when you signed the bill that put a price on my head. My plan worked. I drew in the four men I suspected of being the ones who had killed Charles. But I did not destroy them at once. I spied upon them all in turn until I was certain of their identity as the guilty men. I waited even longer than that. I waited until they were false to me and the gang. Then I killed them, one by one. When they were killed I resigned from my leadership, as you also should know. For my work was done. I went back to the girl of whom I told you. Then, while I was with her, I was arrested by a private detective. You know the rest."

"Mr. Richards, you are accused of a hundred murders, well-nigh."

"Every man who was hurt on the range, if the guilty man was not known, put the blame on The Whisperer. But I have told you the truth."

"No court would believe you."

"That is why I have told it to you."

"Richards, you actually expect to win a pardon from me by telling me this story?"

"Not at all. I am here to show you that I am a human being who made a mistake; I am not a villain. Also, I want you to know that it is possible for me to become a good citizen—to settle down and raise a family. Will you believe that?"

"That may possibly be believed. But you told me that you would drive a bargain with me. What, Richards, can you possibly offer to the State as an inducement to give you a pardon?"

The answer came promptly.

"A cessation from crime!"

"You are mad!"

"Not at all. I have killed only four men. I have never yet profited to the extent of a penny, myself, from any crime which I have committed. But if you turn me back into the mountains again, who knows what will happen? What kept me from running amuck before was the hope that eventually, when my work was done, I could return to live as a peace-loving man. If that hope is taken away from me forever, I'll be apt to turn into a man destroyer."

"Such destroyers are always taken in time."

"But sometimes a long time. Sometimes ten, sometimes twenty years! With me, it might be even longer. I can live without companions to betray me. I have no vices, such as drink or gaming. Why should I not survive, just as I have done before? And, surviving, my gun would talk for me whenever my path had to cross that of other men!"

"Mr. Richards, you could never do that; you are not bloodthirsty enough for that."

"Am I bloodthirsty enough, then, to be hanged?"

"Mr. Whisperer, you talk like a man. But there is only one way that I can be expected to consider your case—not, mind you, to promise you a pardon!"

"Well, sir?"

"Go to prison and await what justice has to say to you. When justice has finished talking, and when I have examined her verdict, if she condemns you, it may be that I shall find grounds to pardon you. It may be that I shall not. But remember—I make no promises, and if I think you guilty, of which there is more than a probability, I would have you killed as readily as I would have a mad dog killed in the streets."

"I shall be content," said the outlaw.

"Then render yourself my prisoner, sir!"

"I shall gladly do it."

"Give me your guns."

They were surrendered.

"Now, walk with me to that house!"

So it was that the governor came in with the greatest prize of the criminal history of that decade. They came in walking shoulder to shoulder, and under the governor's arm, as he walked, were tucked the two long, black guns of the man killer.

Epilogue

Happiness

The Whisperer was convicted. He was voted guilty by the jury without a dissentient voice. But that same jury also strongly recommended that the prisoner be shown mercy because of the strange story which the governor had made public of the outlaw's confession to him. That story had been repeated at the trial. Though a fiery and cunning State attorney had hammered and banged away at the evidence, he could not beat it. From day to day, the people read in the papers the thrilling and strange testimony of this man's life in the wilderness.

There was no doubt about what would happen. The very judge who condemned The

317

Whisperer to be hanged by the neck until he was dead, spoke with a smile. He said to The Whisperer that he was sorry he could not do what the governor would probably see fit to accomplish.

What the governor did, however, was a surprise to every one. For, instead of pardoning the criminal, he offered him a choice of a term of a year's hard labor or death. The labor was accepted and the term was served out.

"Because," said the governor, "if the social State is generous enough to pardon an offender, he must be taught to respect the weight of her hand, just the same."

So The Whisperer served out his term. When he was through, he came out from the jail door, married Rose at the first minister's they could reach, and then went to call on the governor, as soon as he could dodge the multitude of photographers who thronged to try to snap their pictures.

For the crimes of Jack Richards, alias The Whisperer, alias Jeremy Saylor, were soon forgotten. The wild romance of his life was all that was remembered and loved by the people. For, after all, the people by the unit are stern and wise and clever, but the people by the million are simply so many gentle, passionate children, sometimes terrible in cruelty, to be sure, and sometimes just as foolishly sentimental. They chose to make a hero out of Jack Richards and a heroine out of his bride.

The Whispering Outlaw

The governor, when he saw them, apologized to the new Mrs. Richards for keeping her husband away, and then he took Jack into his closet and talked with him long and earnestly. What the governor said to him during that conference could never be learned from Jack, but he came out wearing a perpendicular wrinkle between his eyes; and through the rest of his life he never lost that wrinkle and a certain gravity and sense of care. Had he grown to be old, he would have carried a solemn air into his old age. But no man who had made for himself so many enemies and upon whose head the guilt of so many crimes were wrongly heaped could have expected to survive very long.

The rich rancher, in fact, outlived both his son and his daughter. And he used to tell his grandchildren, in the days that came after, about their wild and magnificent father, and the strange deeds of The Whisperer.

The only part of the story which he failed to repeat was that which concerned his own ridiculous episode in the jail when he had been forced to free his prisoner; an episode, it may be added, which showed the people of the range that their sheriff was not a lion after all, but only a lamb, and a very mild one. They had as much affection for Percival Kenworthy, after that, as they had ever had before. But now, when they thought of him, they were apt to smile a little.

As for Rose and Jack, they were gloriously happy for a few short years. But, after all, is it not true that sometimes one day is as long as a lifetime? For their parts, they were sure that every day together was richer than a life.